THE DEVIL'S SURROGATE

by

JENNIFER JANE POPE

Published by **CHIMERA**
ISBN 9781780806464

Author's Preface

Well, here we are again, back in the seventeenth century, and things are just the same as when we left them some months ago, with our main heroine in a very precarious predicament and a lot of other people variously confused and frustrated by the machinations of our assorted villains. But I promise you, all will be resolved, for good or bad, by the end of this book; no more 'hanging on by the fingernails' open-endings.

To those of you who wrote to me after reading *Cauldron of Fear*... yes, I know it was a bit of a mean trick to leave everything so 'up in the air' like that, yet it was gratifying to know so many of you had enjoyed the book to the extent that you were left chewing on your knuckles. However, I swear it was not my original intention. My books (and I know it happens to other authors as well) have this tendency to assume a life of their own in which events are governed by the developing characters and I end up feeling like little more than an observer recording what happens for the benefit of posterity. In *Cauldron*, this happened to such an extent that... well, we basically ran out of book, and short of chopping everything short in what would have been a most unsatisfactory fashion, or ending up with a volume so thick it would have been nearly impossible to publish, there was nothing else for it but to make this a two book story.

Back on the positive side, it is nice to know so many of you enjoyed *Cauldron of Fear* for reasons other than the most obvious, and especially that you appreciated the historical bits. I do like to be accurate, and yes, I *have* always been a bit of a history buff. That's the main reason I began the *Teena Thyme* series, and now I have the opportunity to bounce our eponymous heroine around through the ages. If you haven't met Teena yet, her first adventure takes her back into early Victorian days, complete with tightly laced corsets, silk stockings, villainous noblemen, and... well, that's another story and the book is out there if you fancy it.

For the moment, we're back in sixteen-sixty. For those of you who may have missed the first volume, there's a bit of background in the following prologues, together with a brief summary of the plot so far. You can skip over both if you wish and probably enjoy this volume just as much, but I think it will be worth a few minutes of your time to do the job properly.

Well, enough of the chat, apart from thanking you all once again for your continued interest and support. Now let's turn the clock back precisely three-hundred and forty-one years...

Prologue I
A Brief History According to the Jenny Pope Annals

The seventeenth century was both a curious century and an important one in that it linked the sixteenth century to the eighteenth century. If that sounds obvious, and even a bit silly, maybe it is worth thinking about the fact that this particular span of one hundred years linked the Elizabethan era to the beginning of what we now can think of as the modern age, and so many things happened in that time that it would take twenty volumes the size of this one to even begin to do the subject justice.

Indeed, at the birth of the seventeenth century, Elizabeth the virgin queen was still on the English throne, albeit in the twilight years of her long life and reign, and by the end of the century the country had executed a king, experienced Parliamentary 'democracy', made great strides towards colonising and 'civilising' great tracts of the globe, and seen the real beginning of the first scientific age, thanks to the enthusiasm and patronage of Charles II when he wasn't bouncing around atop Nell Gwynne and others.

In between times there was the Bubonic Plague, which decimated a large part of the population, and the Great Fire of London, whose origin still gives rise to much debate. Was it a plot by the powers that be to cleanse the capital of the deadly plague virus? We will never know, just as we will never know the real truth behind so many momentous historical events, but then this is not a history book.

What we do know, and what a lot of people forget, is that the Plague epidemic of sixteen sixty-five was not the first time the deadly disease reared its ugly head. For decades there were sporadic and mostly isolated outbreaks, and thousands died prior to the final apocalypse. The church preached that the Plague was a punishment from God, and even hinted that the Plague might be the work of witches, even though the bishops had by now decreed that there was no such thing as witchcraft. Mind you, they had not quite gotten around to actually outlawing the execution of witches as such, but merely declared that perhaps witches did not really exist... perhaps.

It seems crazy to us now looking back from the relative sanity of our own times (and I use the term 'sanity' very advisedly) that on the one hand the church could say witches did not exist, and on the other hand it could still turn a blind eye when some poor young wench or old crone was strung up for allegedly practicing the dark arts. But then we have to understand that these were times of great flux, lacking in the sort of communication we take for granted today. Also, as one contemporary scholar put it, there was a perceived difference between actually *being* a witch (the church said you could not actually be one now) and *practicing* the Satanic arts. The fact that the former had been decreed impossible did not preclude unfortunate souls from being prosecuted and persecuted for still believing it possible. Believing in the black arts was heresy, and this was the crime for which women, and some men, were actually sentenced.

The one fortunate aspect of the situation for the unfortunate victims was that at least by this time England had stopped burning heretics and witches. Hanging, although not yet the relatively instantaneous death it later became when the 'drop' method was universally introduced, was a far preferable and less agonising way of going to meet your Maker. Strangulation may not be nice, but compared to writhing around as your flesh is roasted away... well, enough said, I think.

The 'drop' method of hanging was finally officially introduced and perfected as a method of swift dispatch in the middle to the late nineteenth century, but it was in existence a long time before that and originally employed in places such as Italy and the Balkan States, as we know them now, at least by the more enlightened and compassionate rulers, which made its use rare indeed. I mention this in case some of you are wondering about the fact that its use was touched upon in *Cauldron of Fear* and again in this book.

As for the state of crime, law and order and justice in general, especially in England, it would not be inaccurate to suggest they left a lot to be desired. Cromwell had created the country's first standing army, but as for civilian law enforcement, it was at best hit-or-miss and at worst merely chronic. A patchwork of magistrates, constables, wardens and local militia-style forces had sprung up without any real order or organisation, and were generally run by whoever held the most sway locally. It was a situation ripe for corruption and good-old human nature was not slow to oblige.

It is also worth remembering, at least in order to get this story into some sort of context, that slavery was still legal in this country, as it was in most of the world, and not just the enslavement of non-whites. Europeans could find themselves sold into slavery by courts, whose authority was often quite dubious, for the most trivial offence. Slaves made money, and people with money seldom tended to be content with what they had, not when they could make a lot more money with the aid of a few bought testimonies and a few greedy magistrates and judges. Quite often, in fact, these people *were* the magistrates and judges.

And so, dear reader, armed with this little potted analysis, let us move on now and view the unfolding events in the same dark light that was all-pervasive back then...

Prologue II
The Story So Far
(Note: Please see Cast of Characters Appendix at the end of the book)
From *Cauldron of Fear*

The girl was young, fresh and virginal, even her shaven skull unable to disguise her basic, innocent prettiness. Jacob Crawley, standing in the shadows at the far end of the vault from where she hung chained against the rough stone wall, licked his thin lips in anticipation.

Quietly, with a lightness of step that belied his fifty-something years, he moved closer, until he hovered at the very edge of the pool of orange torchlight that illuminated the captive wench, his black hair and the long black cape he held about his tall frame blending with the darkness behind him and rendering him all but invisible. He saw that her eyes were closed and guessed she was probably fallen into a light sleep of sheer exhaustion, despite the pain her enforced position would be growing in her shoulders and arms, and in the stretched muscles of her calves and thighs as they tried to take some of her weight via the tips of her toes that barely touched the cold floor.

Her breasts, distorted somewhat by her stretched posture, were small and firm, the nipples prominent and deeply coloured, as yet unmarked, per Crawley's strictest instructions. He grinned maliciously to himself, knowing that they would not remain thus for much longer.

Between her taut thighs, her shaven pudenda pouted alluringly, the chains at her ankles holding her legs apart just sufficiently to prevent any attempt at modesty, and Crawley felt a cold shiver of lust crawl slowly up his spine. This one, he thought, was far too good to waste on the scaffold, far too sweet a fruit to plant in the chill earth beyond the consecrated ground of the churchyard. No, he chuckled, this one would not be broken, though he knew she would probably require a taste of his own peculiar skills and more than a modicum of bending before she would be totally satisfactory.

Not that the process would take that long; it seldom did. Two days, three at the most. Three days that would to her, however, pass like a millennium, so that when Crawley finally granted her even the smallest measure of relief and the chance to avoid the fate to which she would by then have consigned herself and probably even craved, she would take it gratefully, no matter to what level of degradation she must surely know she would sink.

Crawley shuffled his position, the muscles in his right thigh having stiffened in the damp air, and the slight sound brought the girl immediately awake again, her wide brown eyes flickering from side to side in alarm.

'Who... who's there?' she cried, her voice thin and wavering in her terror of the unknown. 'Please,' she wailed, when Crawley made no reply nor moved to reveal himself, 'please, whoever you are, take pity. I am no witch; surely you must all know that by now. Ask in the village, as I said, everyone will tell you.'

'Oh, people always tell me what they think I will believe,' Crawley replied, breaking his silence at last, though still remaining back from the light, 'at least in the beginning.' His voice betrayed his north country roots, though many years had softened the harsher edges of his accent. 'Satan woos his brides to proliferate his evil lies, but the Good Lord has bestowed on me the gift of cutting through them.'

'Sir!' Tears welled up in the girl's eyes and began trickling down cheeks that were already stained. 'Sir, I am no bride of the devil, nor do I lie. I fear God and worship our saviour and a more devout girl you will surely never find.'

'You are Matilda Pennywise, of the Parish of St Jude?'

The girl nodded, swallowing hard.

Crawley inched forward, so that his outline was now visible to her, but only as a deeper shadow. 'Speak girl,' he commanded. 'Are you, or are you not, Matilda Pennywise?'

'Yes!' Matilda gasped. 'Yes sir, indeed I am... sir,' she added as an afterthought.

'That's better, wench,' Crawley cackled, 'you seem to be learning something at last.' He coughed, clearing his throat. 'Then, Matilda Pennywise,' he continued after a carefully judged pause, 'you stand accused of several counts of witchcraft, sorcery and consorting with unholy forces.'

'No!' Matilda shrieked. 'No, it's all lies, as God is my witness!'

Without warning Crawley leapt forward, his right arm swinging in a wide arc, the open palm of his hand slapping into the girl's unprotected cheek with such force that she would have been knocked off her feet were the chains not holding her upright. She let out a howl of pain, not least because the full weight of her body had momentarily been transferred to her already tortured upper limbs.

'Silence!' he roared. 'Heresy, to invoke the name of the Lord God you have betrayed.' Matilda was struggling to regain her balance and clearly scarcely heard him, but Crawley knew his words would sink in eventually. 'You are all the same, you Devil's spawn harlots, every single one of you,' he intoned. 'Yet I shall save your unholy soul, mark my words. You will return to the arms of the heavenly master cleansed of your foul wickedness, else my name be not Jacob Crawley!'

The main action of the story takes place in and around the fictitious village of Leddingham, near the border between the counties of Hampshire and Surrey, set on what is now known as the main A3, the road from London to the great naval port of Portsmouth on the south coast. The local inn, *The Black Drum*, owned by Thomas Handiwell, does a brisk trade from both travellers and locals alike.

Just to the north and west of Leddingham lies the huge Grayling estate, run in the absence of his father, Earl Grayling, by the cruel and manipulative Roderick, who has built up a lucrative business in white slaving, concentrating mostly on young women trained at the Hall by his strict overseers and then sold on to all parts of the world.

A little south of Grayling Hall is the much smaller farm estate of Barten Meade, owned by Oliver Merridew, a former army major now virtually bedridden as a result of wounds sustained during his military career. The impoverished farm is kept going by Harriet, his pretty and intelligent daughter, but times are so hard that she is beginning to consider the marriage proposals she has received from the widowed Master Handiwell. He is unaware his affection for her has triggered a terrible hatred in his daughter, Jane, who sees Harriet as a threat to her inheritance and who is also terribly jealous that she was not blessed with the same fine looks.

A would-be witch, Jane has recruited a small band of highwaywomen, including Roderick Grayling's younger sister Ellen, and this foursome have terrified the night roads, robbing coaches and abducting any suitable young females to sell to Roderick. Into this trap comes Sarah Merridew, Harriet's cousin, recently orphaned in London after a local plague outbreak and now seeking the sanctuary of her only remaining relatives.

Meanwhile, Jacob Crawley has arrived in the village, a brooding, menacing figure who carries with him a written authority appointing him as a *witchfinder*, even though the church supposedly abandoned such practices more than a decade earlier. Crawley has been summoned by the local minister, Simon Wickstanner, whose spurned advances toward a young local girl, Matilda Pennywise, have turned to thoughts of revenge spurred on by the rumours that Matilda's grandmother, Hannah, is hoarding a small fortune amassed by her own father, Nathan, now dead many long years.

With a dubious signed testimony by a local labourer, who has since mysteriously died, Crawley arrests Matilda and subjects her to a horrifying ordeal whose purpose he alleges is to draw a confession from her as well as to purge her of her sins. However, when he attempts to persuade Hannah to pay penance in gold to save Matilda from the scaffold, he is astonished to be met with outright refusal.

Thomas Handiwell has meantime set off for London in an attempt to persuade the army to send men to help him search for the abducted Sarah, while the resourceful Harriet has recruited the assistance of young Toby Blaine and his friends to try to help her discover who is behind the kidnapping. Unfortunately, although she succeeds in uncovering some of the identities of the perpetrators, she herself is captured when she attempts to pay a ransom, and is substituted by the vengeful Jane for Matilda and left in the crypt of the church, naked, hooded and gagged, and surely soon to be hanged before Crawley or his assistants have the chance to discover her true identity.

Thomas Handiwell has meantime returned to Leddingham, completely unaware that the hand behind the now double abduction is that of his own daughter, Jane.

'Our methods are now well and truly tried and tested, Sir Peregrine,' Adam Portfield said smugly. He always enjoyed escorting prospective clients around the estate; delighted in showing off the training techniques he and his fellow overseers utilised, secure in the knowledge that his employer, Sir Roderick Grayling, would have vetted these visitors most thoroughly before permitting them access to this, his most closely guarded citadel.

Today's visitor, Sir Peregrine Wellthorne, was younger than most. The sort of money the Grayling enterprise commanded for its human products tended to be beyond the reach of all but the most wealthy and such wealth usually took time to accumulate. Sir Wellthorne looked to be in his early thirties, although his flushed countenance suggested a lifestyle not conducive to longevity. Wellthorne had inherited his father's shipping fortunes when the old man had, unfortunately, gone down aboard one of his merchantmen during an unseasonable storm in the Channel. Peregrine had since proceeded to employ much of his wealth in ways that would have had his father turning in his grave, had they ever been able to recover his body and give it the luxury of one, that is.

'Yes, I'm sure you know what you're doing, Mister Portfield,' Sir Wellthorne drawled, his eyes bulging slightly as two buxom females appeared in the doorway at the end of the long barn, naked except for stringent leather harnesses and matching leather hoods that completely obscured their features. Behind them, a young and lanky sandy-haired fellow cracked a heavy whip. The wicked thong missed the girls' defenceless shoulders by mere fractions of an inch, but the sharp report made them flinch nonetheless.

'Tell me, though,' he continued, swivelling his head to watch the progress of the glistening bodies with their bouncing bosoms, 'why the hood thing? Don't want your clients to see what they're buying, is that it?'

Adam smiled, but kept his face turned away so that his companion could not see his amusement. It was the usual question, after all, and few visitors understood without having it explained to them, sometimes more than once, and then there were still those who were unable to grasp the concept. 'The girls are slaves now,' Adam said very slowly and deliberately. 'They all come from different backgrounds - city streets, country lanes, and even, sometimes, from quite comfortable circumstances. The only thing they have in common is that they are comely, young, fit and pleasing to the eye. Once they arrive here, however, they have everything and one thing in common, the only thing that counts, namely that they are now slaves and have no will, or choice, of their own. Neither will a pretty face or a pleading smile avail them, not while they are kept hooded, as you see most of them now. By hiding their faces we submerge their individualities, indeed their very personalities. They soon come to understand that now they are seen as only one thing, a means of gratification and service to their masters and mistresses to be. Here we view them only as one might view any other livestock. A farmer doesn't value his cows by the prettiness of their faces, after all!'

Sir Peregrine guffawed and nodded enthusiastically. 'Indeed not! A good point, and well made, sir. Though a good brood mare may oft times be judged by the lines of her muzzle and not just by her flanks.'

'Which is why we always give our buyers every opportunity to view the goods properly before buying,' Adam said. 'Meantime, however, we keep the bitches masked and their hair shorn, so that even when they are not wearing the hood for bathing they all feel as if they look alike. Besides, for those we send abroad, the lack of hair is an advantage when it comes to ensuring they don't become flea-ridden during the long voyage.'

Sir Peregrine retorted, laughing, 'Well, a few fleabites never hurt a wench, that's for sure! But I daresay you fellows know your trade.'

'Indeed we do,' Adam muttered. 'The easier it is to keep our cargoes clean, the more of them survive to reach their destinations. Lost stock is lost money, Sir Peregrine, and I was raised to abhor waste in any shape or form.'

'Well, I must say, the shapes and forms about here are most pleasing.' Peregrine leered as another pair of hooded and harnessed slaves appeared at the end of the barn, followed by an even younger groom. These two girls were very pale-skinned; evidently their bodies had never been exposed to the elements.

'These two,' Adam said, noting Peregrine's renewed interest, 'come from the north, probably from the Norse lands. They were purchased cheaply from a Scandinavian sea captain who needed money to affect some urgent repairs to his vessel after a storm forced him to turn into Harrogate two weeks since.'

'But you'll not be offering them on so cheaply, I'll venture.'

'Business is business, Sir Peregrine,' Adam smiled at him again. 'Besides, the prices are none of my business. Sir Roderick sees to that side himself.'

'When he's not got one or another of his little *piccaninnies* sucking on the end of his cock, that is?' Peregrine sniffed, and then let out a raucous laugh. 'Damned if I can see what he finds so attractive in that pair of black wenches. Not one of them stands any higher than this!' He raised a hand to about the level of his heart. 'Probably only keeps them because nobody else would pay good money for such freaks!'

Adam refused to be drawn out. Like Sir Peregrine, he found little he considered attractive in the two diminutive African girls, but then he knew that tastes varied, and he was not about to decry those of his employer, who very much enjoyed the doglike devotion and willing mouths of Popsy and Topsy, and would not willingly swap them even for the most alluring white beauty. 'Perhaps you see something you might like to sample yourself? With our compliments, of course,' he suggested, deftly changing the course of the discussion. 'We have several girls now who are suitably broken, and they're all clean enough once we sluice the dust of the day off them. Perhaps I could show you some possibilities and then offer you some refreshments while the lads prepare your choice?'

Harriet recognised the gaunt figure of Jacob Crawley even in the near darkness of the crypt room into which she had been cast by Jane Handiwell's cohorts, but she knew he would not have recognised her even if the room had been bathed in bright sunlight. The thick leather mask concealed her identity completely, and the barbarous spike from the metal cage that had been locked onto her head over the hood dug viciously into her tongue every time she tried to move it, making intelligible speech completely impossible.

'Ah, dear little Matilda,' he grunted, stooping over her prone figure and reaching out a bony hand to stroke her naked left breast. 'What a shame to waste such youthful perfection, but the work of the Lord allows little room for personal gratification or preferences.'

The man was clearly insane. Harriet was sure now of what she had already suspected as she saw the strange light burning deep in his eyes. That he would assume she was Matilda was no surprise, but that he could pretend, let alone evidently believe, his evil actions were even remotely excusable or connected with religion proved to her beyond a shadow of a doubt that he was completely mad. However, mad or not, she was now totally in his power, and judging from what she had heard from the villagers, in imminent danger of her life.

'I have decided to allow a little more time for that witch, your grandmother, to see sense,' he growled, his fingers moving to her other breast.

Harriet felt her stomach tighten and her blood turn to ice in her veins, but knew there was little point in risking antagonising this lunatic further by trying to draw away from his touch.

'The old woman has sent word that she wishes to barter,' Crawley continued, his lip curling back in a grin that revealed misshapen, yellowing teeth. 'I sense she is simply trying to buy time and seeking to trick me. However,' he muttered, 'one of the village men tells me he saw her with the young Calthorpe lad, which may well explain the apparent disappearance of my man, Jed Mardley. The crone is planning something, I can feel it, but if she thinks to outwit me, she'll live to regret it, if only briefly. Jed tells me that dropping you whore-spawn on the end of a rope makes for a painless end, but it also makes for a quick one with no time for intervention. I discovered, many years ago, that even the most cowardly soul may be stirred to action by the sight of a loved one dancing on the end of a gallows rope, but with this new way there is no time. Jed pulls his lever, and *bang*, down you go.' He snapped his fingers and cackled to himself. 'Just like that, the neck is broken and you're no more than carrion. Not so much as a twitching toe, Matilda, dear.' He moved his other hand up to the side of her neck, fingering the narrow steel band that kept the old scold's bridle from being removed. 'This is even thin enough that it won't interfere with the rope,' he snickered, 'so you'll meet your death with nothing more than a garbled whimper. No witching curses from the scaffold from you, my dear child, no indeed.'

He straightened up, and with an awkward gesture managed to throw his cape from his shoulders, letting it cascade to the floor behind him in a crumpled heap. 'But that is all for later, my precious.' He fumbled with the buckle of his belt. 'Now that most of the devil's work has been scourged from you, it's time again to at least welcome your physical body back into the fold.' He drew the front of his breeches apart and Harriet saw that his shaft was already growing erect. To her horrified astonishment, she saw also that it appeared to be inordinately long, making it appear thinner than she might have expected, like the neck of a rearing serpent. 'Let's see if you still have the strength to wriggle as you did before,' he challenged, leering. 'Up on your feet now, whore girl, and let us dance together!'

Kitty realised resignedly that she was now even beginning to think of herself by her new name. Miranda Parkes, after all, belonged in a world so different from the one in which she now found herself that she would probably have killed herself rather than submit to the appalling indignities now inflicted upon her with such cold detachment. It was easier to imagine she was indeed Titty Kitty, and that she had lived no other life before this.

As she trotted dutifully along - wrists bound tightly in the small of her back, waist cinched by the cruel girth strap, her breasts bouncing, their size exaggerated by the thin leather bands that had been drawn tightly around them at their base - the *crack-crack* of the whip seemed to echo inside her head as if from another world, its sound muffled by the restraining hood encasing her smoothly shaven head. Alongside her trotted a similarly garbed girl, distinguishable from Kitty only by the fact that her breasts were considerably smaller, whilst behind her she could imagine the cool yet interested expression of their groom, the ginger-haired Ross who had taken over her training now that the man Adam seemed to have lost his earlier interest in her.

Perhaps, she mused, chewing on the wad of leather that served as an immovable gag inside her hood, the fact that Ross himself seemed far more interested in the newly arrived Sarah might mean that she, Kitty, would get an easier time of it for a few days, but she was not pinning any hopes on that. The men who ran this terrible place all seemed to have an insatiable appetite for their charges - they were all so young and undeniably fit, as she had seen immediately - and seemed able to go from one to another with barely a break in between.

At least, she sighed to herself, they weren't superhuman and she had eventually been allowed to rest when they finally retired to wherever it was they slept, although Ross had reappeared at dawn to stir them from their slumbers and curse and kick them back into consciousness. Kitty risked a covert glance to her left, peering sideways through the vision-restricting slits in her hood, in an effort to see how her companion was faring. There was little to indicate Sarah's state, the leather-masked features betraying nothing, her breathing as laboured through her nostrils as was her own.

'Eyes front, whore!' The whip cracked out again, but this time the tip caught Kitty exactly between her shoulder blades and she leapt, a sharp squeal of pain forcing its way past her gag. *Damn him!* she cursed in her head, her eyes burning with tears, for it had only been the briefest of glances and she could have sworn she had not even turned her head, certainly not more than the merest fraction of an inch.

'Pick it up there now!' Ross snapped. 'Let's see those bubbies bounce. Or shall I get some bells to hang on those teat rings?'

Kitty blinked to clear her vision and desperately tried to obey, for the thought of anything being hung onto the rings that now adorned her recently pierced nipples was almost too much to bear. Ross had demonstrated the previous evening just how painful even the smallest tug could be, and how by means of even two of the thinnest leather thongs attached to the twin metal circles a man could exert total control over her.

'That's better!'

Kitty stifled a sigh of relief. At least for the moment she was to be spared that indignity, though she knew there would be others and that it would not be long before one of the men, even if it were not Ross himself, would take advantage of her helplessness. Both she and Sarah had been brought out without thick dildos strapped into them, and Kitty had discovered this meant only that their sexes were being left that much more available for a human phallus.

'Left now... left, I say!' Ross flicked the whip in an arc that allowed it to merely kiss both sets of shoulders. 'There!' he cried. 'There, onto that path, you idle sluts. Let's get some blood running in those legs and pussies.' The ground beneath their bare feet began to rise slightly, but even this gentle gradient imposed considerable extra strain upon muscles that were already screaming in protest.

This way, Kitty now knew, lay two smaller barns which the grooms used to house their charges on some nights when the main barn was particularly crowded, or when they decided it was time to impose some particularly wicked discipline on certain of their charges. Both buildings had been equipped with a bewildering array of punishment and torture devices, ranging from simple trestles - upon which a girl could be painfully mounted - to stocks and pillories that must have tested the ingenuity of their designers, and which could be employed to secure a victim in almost any position of pain, degradation and availability for either punishment or sexual gratification.

She sucked in as deep a breath as the constricting girth would permit and ground her teeth into her gag. At least, she tried to console herself, whatever indignity their coldly efficient trainer decided to inflict upon them, it could be no worse than this constant trotting uphill with lungs already threatening to burst and sweat now pouring from every pore of their bodies. Also, she had discovered almost immediately upon her arrival, the pain and indignity would eventually become partially assuaged by the waves of pleasure even such inhuman treatment somehow managed to generate in her treacherous body.

Jacob Crawley gripped the writhing girl's buttocks hard with his bony fingers, delighting in the way her body squirmed helplessly against his own, and in the deep heat gripping his throbbing member as she hung impaled upon it, her bare toes inches off the stone floor, her legs kicking helplessly as she strove to free herself; a fruitless struggle, for he had her firmly and would not release her until he had sated himself.

'Bitch... whore...' he hissed. 'Try to seduce the Lord's appointed hand with your lewdness, would you?' He barely suppressed a chuckle, for even his warped mind knew well enough that Matilda's desperate twisting and turning was no attempt to stir his lust but merely the instinctive struggling of a trapped creature, the way a fly might twitch and twist in the helpless grip of a spider's web.

He moved one hand up, pressing against the small of her back so her naked breasts were crushed against his own bare chest. The smell of her was overpowering; sweat, fear, and yes, even that smell of lust. These ungodly sluts simply could not help themselves. Weakness, the weakness that was woman incarnate, the same weakness that had led Eve to sample the forbidden fruit, and all at the behest of a serpent. Now another serpent was summoning this Eve's whore, the stiff serpent that sprang up from his loins and upon which she was now so totally impaled, repenting and repaying the treachery of her sex to the Lord God their maker. Crawley ground his broken teeth hard together, feeling the first waves of his own surrender beginning to build, knowing he must soon spurt his seed deep into her faithless womb and yet wishing to prolong the moment of deep, agonising ecstasy for both of them.

'Bitch...' he groaned, butting his head against the leather covering of her cheek, forgetting the steel band that crossed it and yet oblivious to the pain as his forehead slammed into it. 'Bitch!' he roared again, and holding her writhing body even tighter, exploded a torrent of semen into her with a ferocity that threatened to buckle his own legs beneath their combined weight.

Very dimly, Sarah Merridew was aware that something had happened inside her head, something she could not explain and yet something for which, in a curious way, she was grateful.

It was as if some part of her brain had simply shut down by refusing to accept that any of this could actually be happening to her. Now she found herself blessed with the ability to experience everything as if it was happening to someone else, as if she was viewing it all dispassionately through a smeared and smoky glass. It was not as if she could do anything about it anyway. These terrible people, whoever they were, had seen to it that she was kept in a state of total helplessness ever since they seized her, wasting no time in reducing her to a condition that was at best animalistic, and at worst...

She peered down through the eye slits in her hood at her breasts, which bobbed up and down as she trotted dutifully along, the early morning sun occasionally glinting on the metal rings that now hung from just below each of her nipples. They really did look quite pretty, she mused, and then castigated herself fiercely for entertaining such a thought. It was one thing to accept a certain inevitability about her situation, but quite another to consider it anything but terrible. And for a young lady to even enjoy the sight of her bared bosom, especially one that had been handled in such a crude and summary fashion, had to be a sin on a level no Christian woman could begin to contemplate.

So why did her nipples tingle so pleasantly in the fresh, warm breeze? Why did she continue to feel that heat deep inside her groin, the same heat the brutal Ross had kindled and which refused to cool even though she had since managed a few hours of very uncomfortable sleep? Why did she, knowing that Ross would soon be thrusting into her again, not view the prospect with terror and abhorrence? Why, she was forced to ask herself, did she feel almost as if she were looking forward to it?

'Damn all of them to hell!' Thomas Handiwell slammed his tankard down onto the bar of the *Black Drum* and glared at the small assembled company. 'Call themselves men and talk about freedom, yes,' he sneered, 'but ask any one of them to go against their so-called lords and masters, even when we have evidence of their guilt, and they run and hide their faces!'

'My men report that at least four of them have joined up with this Crawley fellow,' Captain Timothy Hart said quietly. 'It would seem they respond to gold rather better than they do to duty, but then I cannot really blame them, those who'll not join us, that is. The Graylings are a rich and powerful family, by all accounts, and they doubtless have rich and powerful friends.'

'Aye, that they are, and that they surely do,' Handiwell muttered, 'but I'm damned if I'll stand by and let any man's supposed birthright or wealth flout basic laws and human standards. They can't simply snatch innocent people from the roads as if they were no better than common slaves!'

'And what of your friend, this Mistress Merridew?' Hart enquired, blinking his watery eyes as the first shaft of sunlight suddenly penetrated through the east facing window like a bright sword shaft thrusting into the gloomy barroom. 'Should we not have heard something from her by now? I fear they may have taken her as well.'

'Damn the foolish wench,' Handiwell snapped, but there was a note of tender concern in his oath. 'I warned her against the venture, and warned her to stay back and run if there was trouble.'

'Maybe she tried and simply could not run fast enough,' Hart suggested.

Sergeant Paddy Riley nodded, sagely. 'Ain't easy fer a lady to run fast in skirts, and not that much better if'n she wears breeches, I'd say. Running ain't woman's work, that's what my ma used to tell me, anyway.'

'Thank you, sergeant,' Hart retorted a bit acidly, 'your homespun family philosophy and wit are hardly called for here, I think.'

'Maybe not, sir,' Riley replied, unabashed by the intended rebuke, 'but there's maybe a few homespun skills that would be welcome. Sean Kelly and meself could get ourselves in there, I reckon, unless they've got a whole regiment of those bastards wandering around the woods.'

'And what good could two of you do?' Hart asked impatiently. 'All that would likely happen is you'd get caught, or shot, and that would leave me with two less men. We've already lost Hollis. Isn't that bad enough?'

'Certainly it's bad, captain sir,' Riley said. 'I've known Hollis since he first joined up, as it happens, and a nicer lad you couldn't wish for, not even when he was in his cups, but that's a soldier's lot and we all accept it when we take the shilling. On the other hand, sir,' he continued, leaning forward in his chair, 'maybe this Grayling place isn't quite the ground for ordinary soldiering, eh? No self-respecting general would commit his troops into woods like those, not when every tree and every bush could be hiding a musket primed and ready. No, captain, begging your pardon, there's a time and a place for everything, and a reason for some, and woods were made for poaching, just as sure as me name is Patrick Michael Flaherty Riley.'

'And just as sure as you probably grew up feeding your family on rabbits that didn't belong to you, sergeant?' Handiwell interjected, quite unable to keep the grin from his face despite the gravity of the situation. 'Kelly too, perhaps?'

'Without it we'd have all starved, and without being caught I reckon neither of us would be in this damned army, begging your pardon, sir,' Riley retorted, but his own grin belied the supposed apology in his words. 'The two of us could slip in there, I reckon, though we'd need to be borrowing some more suitable clothing. These damned tunics are far too bright. Something nice and drab would do the job, I think.'

'I'll see what I can find for you,' Handiwell said without waiting for further comment from Hart. 'Meantime, perhaps Anne would be so good as to see what might be available for breaking our fast. This could be yet another long day, if I'm any judge of these things, and it could be many a long hour before any of us gets the chance to eat again, at least when it comes to a decent hot meal.'

Paddy Riley nodded. 'It might also be a good idea if we took the young Blaine boy along with us,' he suggested. 'He seems to know this country better than most know the back of their hands.'

'But he's only a scrap of a lad!' Anne Billings protested, halting in the doorway on her way to the kitchen.

'But a cunning wee lad, to be sure,' Riley said. 'Believe me, young Toby will be more use than a whole company of troopers out there in those woods and he's less likely to come to any harm than either Kelly or meself. The boy's a survivor if ever there was one, and believe me mistress, it takes one to know one.'

To the surprise of both Hannah Pennywise and James Calthorpe, the little side door of the church was unlocked and the handle turned easily in the old woman's grasp. She looked back at the young man's petrified face, and grinned. 'Careless of the bastards, I'd say,' she declared in a harsh whisper, 'but we'd better go careful, nonetheless. It may be some sort of trap. That Crawley devil is no fool even if Wickstanner is, and his sort don't go around leaving doors

15

unlocked as should be locked, not by mistake, anyways.'

James gripped the unfamiliar weight of the pistol in his right hand and swallowed hard as he tried to stop himself from trembling. 'Perhaps I should go first,' he volunteered gallantly. 'I've got this, after all.'

'And I've got this one, don't forget,' Hannah muttered, drawing the smaller pistol from beneath her shawl and shaking her head. 'No, you stay behind me, my young lad. The world won't miss one more old woman, but it hasn't got so many bright young men it can afford to waste one so willingly, and while my Matilda will no doubt mourn my passing, in the long run she'd mourn yours more. Besides,' she grinned, 'while they're wasting time trying to pot me, it'll give you a chance to take proper aim, and I daresay you can shoot straighter than me?'

'Um, well, I don't know,' James stammered. 'I mean, I've shot a pistol before, of course, but never, well, never at anything that was alive and moving.'

Hannah's eyebrows lifted. 'What, not even a rabbit? No, I suppose not. Too many hours at your schooling I reckon, and a father with no need to put free meat on the table. Ah well,' she sighed, 'just you make sure and take good aim when the time comes. Make sure your first shot counts because you won't have time for a second. And don't,' she added grimly, 'try shooting the bastard in the head. Far too small a target, and it can move too quickly. Aim about here.' She prodded James so fiercely in his stomach that he let out an involuntary gasp. 'Then, if you aim too low,' she chuckled, 'you'll like as not shoot his bollocks off. Stomach or balls, it's all the same, and when one of them goes down making all sorts of noise, the others, if they're there, get less brave, and maybe that'll give us time to reload.'

'You seem to know a lot about these things, Mistress Pennywise,' James said falteringly.

Hannah grimaced and winked up at him. 'These eyes have seen a sight too many things over the years, and this head has maybe taken in at least twice as many as ought to be good for a person's sanity. Now, enough of this talk and let's see what's skulking on the other side of this here door, shall we?'

Slumped into the corner of the damp smelling crypt chamber, Harriet fought desperately to shut out the images and recollections of the way in which Crawley had used her, and the way in which, when he had spent himself, he had simply discarded her like an unwanted jacket and strode from the room. Perhaps death would be far preferable to this horror, she thought. The brute had said the way in which he and his men hanged their victims was quick and painless, although how he could be certain of the latter assertion she had no way of knowing. Yet even death by slow strangulation had to be better than this death of a different kind, the slow and tortuous murder of all her beliefs and values.

With a groan that became a sharp gasp as the wicked metal barb dug into her tongue, Harriet forced herself up into a sitting position. Her wrists were once

16

again shackled at either side of the thick waist belt, but her arms were of little more use to her now than when they had been fastened behind her back. Her ankles remained shackled by the short chain, which had now been attached by means of a length of thick rope to a heavy ring set into the stonework a few feet from where she sat.

Above her head pale light managed to filter in through the narrow and grimy strip of glass, glowing green as it forced its way past the weeds and grass which grew up against it on the outside, so that the entire chamber took on a spectral atmosphere that was as depressing as it was frightening. Somewhere out there lay the real world, the world Harriet knew and which, until such a short time ago, held as its worst prospect a marriage to Thomas Handiwell to save Barten Meade from bankruptcy, and her father from the poor house hospital the army had set up with so much trumpeting, but which Parliament had failed to maintain with sufficient funding. Now, it seemed, if she ever got out of this horror chamber, all that was left her was to stumble naked in her chains to Crawley's scaffold, to die as Matilda Pennywise at the hands of a perverted rogue, probably to the jeering accompaniment of most of the village men folk. If only, she prayed, there was any way she could let someone, even Crawley himself, know of this awful travesty and tell people that this was not even a mistake but a deliberate act by Thomas Handiwell's own daughter. The world had gone mad. Greed and fear, superstition and myth - what price now the bright new age of reason? What price now on the life of a poor wench whose only sin had been to miss church in order to care for a sick father and a struggling farm?

'By the eyes of Hester, what devil's work is this?' The sight that greeted them in the main church visibly stunned Hannah Pennywise, not known for being a woman who was easily shocked.

James Calthorpe put out a hand to steady her, at the same time waving the pistol in a defensive arc about them. Nothing moved, however, and the thick walls and glass meant that even the sounds of the morning birdsong failed to penetrate the oppressive silence. James let out a long breath and took a faltering step forward, his eyes growing larger and rounder as he stared down at the corpse.

The black cassock and the long and slender, almost feminine, fingers told him the body was that of the minister, Simon Wickstanner. Apart from that, it could have been the corpse of any priest, for where there should have been a head there was now only the ripped and bloodied stump of a neck, the pool of blood covering the stone floor in all directions emphasising the fact that the head had not been removed easily or cleanly.

'Monsters!' Hannah breathed. 'The dark ones have sent for their revenge, make no mistake about it!' To James's surprise, the old woman crossed herself and closed her eyes, her lips moving in a silent prayer.

'No,' he announced, regaining some semblance of composure. 'No, this is not

17

the work of any monster, not unless you count the monster who now lies dead before us. Look, Mistress Pennywise.' He jabbed a wavering finger at the ladder, and pointed up to where the rope dangled, a small and bloodied noose at its lower end.

Hannah eventually forced her eyes open again, and gazed upwards. 'What...?' she began, but then a light began to dawn in her eyes. 'But how...?' she muttered.

James shook his head as if in bewilderment, but his educated and fertile brain was already deducing. 'Suicide,' he breathed. 'The bastard hanged himself!'

'But where's his damned head?' Hannah looked wildly about them.

James grunted. 'It'll be here somewhere.' He stared upwards trying to picture the scene. 'The fool tried to make his end quick,' he muttered. 'There's an execution method known as "the drop", in which they drop the victim and the jerk of the rope snaps the neck, killing him instantly. Only, if they make the drop too long...' his voice trailed off.

'He made it far too long then, by the looks of it,' Hannah grasped the implication of James's statement with a turnabout leap that staggered him. 'Ripped his fool head clean off... except it ain't that clean.' She turned to grasp James by the arm, her bony fingers digging into his flesh through his thin jacket. 'We have to go! Come lad, let's get out of here!'

'But what about Matilda?'

Hannah hesitated. 'Not now,' she urged, pulling him back with surprising strength. 'If she *is* still here, there'll be locked doors for sure, and Crawley and his damned murdering henchman won't be that far away, but we cannot risk being found here like this. 'Tis one thing to shoot that black-hearted bastard if he tried to cheat us on the ransom, but another to be found here with a dead priest, no matter how wicked that priest might have been in life. Nay lad, I tell ye, we'll court more trouble than even I can face down if they find us like this. Better to run now and let someone else make the discovery. Besides,' she added, her eyes narrowing, 'even Crawley won't risk trying to hang my Matilda just yet, not once news of this gets out. Folks around here are a lot of things they shouldn't be, and aren't much of what a body might wish them to be, but at least they're respectful, so they won't go along with no hanging, not until they've given this sod a decent Christian burial, whether or not he deserves it.'

'But she may be only a few steps from where we stand now,' James protested.

Hannah nodded, but her resolve was as firm as ever. 'Aye, like as not she is, and there she'll stay, at least for now. We get ourselves into a fight with Crawley meantime, and he'll find a way to blame us for all this mess. People say I'm a witch, and when blood flows and vicars start jumping off ladders with ropes around their scrawny gizzards, well, someone has to be at fault and I knows only too well who'll be first up for the blame, believe you me!'

'Just a few minutes, please!' James begged, but the old woman was adamant.

'No,' she hissed, 'not now. Come on, you young idiot. Remember what they say, "he who runs away, lives to fight another day".'

'But surely that should be, "he who fights and—"'

'Bollocks! Go tell your own grandma to suck eggs, but leave this old woman to know what she knows and just get the hell out of here while we still can!'

Ross McDonald considered himself a Scot, even though his parents had left the land of his birth when he was but a few months old and he had never since returned there. He also considered himself a very fortunate young man, being paid to do a job he knew many of his contemporaries would have volunteered to do for free. However, he was also certain of one very important thing - very few men could have performed his duties quite as efficiently as he did, and neither could they maintain the air of detachment that was the essential ingredient in a good slave handler and trainer.

No matter how beautiful the female, no matter how pitiful or how brash even, Ross treated them all in the same fashion; maintaining a rigid discipline within himself he was then able to impose upon his charges. Even when he finally took a girl - be it for the umpteenth time, or be it an actual deflowering as had been the case with this new arrival, Sarah - he did it primarily as he did everything else, and only when he had begun to take his victim down to depths she had previously never known existed, then and only then might he permit himself the luxury of actually enjoying the act.

He smiled contentedly to himself as the second barn came into view through the thinning screen of trees. The building had lain derelict for many years and its restoration had been Ross's idea, and then his personal project, carried out with the enthusiastic backing of his employer, Roderick Grayling. The furthest structure from Grayling Hall itself, and still more than a mile-and-a-half from the nearest estate boundary, this *Conditioning Centre* - as Ross had himself named it - was still the object of some mockery by his fellow trainers, or at least by those of them who had yet to put its facilities to the proper test.

The C.C. had to be used properly; it was a waste of time bringing the girls out here for just a few hours and then returning them to the main barn, where they would once again be accompanied by their peers and the general hubbub of their shared misery in surroundings that, if not exactly comfortable, would at least have begun to take on a familiar and reassuring atmosphere. As far as Ross was concerned, that reassurance had to be earned, and would be all the more appreciated when a girl had spent at least two or three days in the isolation of his centre subjected to the various devices his peculiarly inventive Scottish mind had created.

After a protracted session in the C.C., even the most truculent slave would become docile and cooperative. Even girls who had been raised in the most affluent circumstances would willingly crawl on their knees and abase themselves in all manner of potentially profitable ways to avoid repeating the experience. A prudent Scot if ever there was one, and a man not given to wasting time any more than he was given to wasting money, Ross exposed each newcomer to a short session in the C.C. However, a prolonged spell in this centre was always eventually necessary, as had been the case with Kitty.

After the short session, when the girl returned to the main establishment, his expert eye soon told him which captive would need further full conditioning and which one was already so chastened by even that short exposure that her training would continue without trouble. There was little point in any of his charges trying to fool him in this respect, and he was also never fooled by a temporary state of shock.

Titty Kitty, despite her apparent willingness to slip into her new role, was a case in point. Yes, she would already go down on her knees and use her mouth to bring any man to arousal and orgasm, and she would apparently enjoy using her generous tits to masturbate anyone who told her to, yet she still retained a streak of individuality no master could tolerate in a pleasure slave.

Now the other girl, Sarah... Ross sighed, and then smiled. Yes, this one was a different kettle of fish entirely. A demure virgin upon her arrival, even his rough deflowering had failed to elicit the sort of terrified reaction expected of girls of her class and upbringing. Instead, she seemed to have slipped away into another world, into a trancelike existence where little seemed able to penetrate.

Was it all an act? He shook his head, unable to decide as he watched her beautifully rounded buttocks and wide hips swaying before him. If it *was* an act, then she was a very good actress indeed, but a day or so in the C.C., two or three days, if necessary, would determine if she was good enough.

Oh yes, there was little chance of Mistress Sarah Merridew being able to pull the wool over his eyes once he had her inside his centre, and if she was pretending it wouldn't matter anyway, for by the time he brought her out again she would certainly not be acting. He had yet to fail in the few months since the inception of his experiment, and he did not expect to begin failing now.

'Dead, you say?' Thomas Handiwell peered at Ned Blaine as if he were having difficulty seeing him clearly, his red-rimmed eyes betraying both his lack of sleep and his mounting concern.

'Aye,' Ned replied, eyeing the shelf behind the bar with ill-concealed interest, for news of such import was certainly worth a generous shot of either rum or brandy. 'Mary Slane found him not half an hour since. Went in to do her turn on the cleaning, and ran out wailing like the wind through the trees of hell, so they say.'

'More foul play?' Handiwell voiced the question aloud although he was talking more to himself.

'They say it was suicide,' Ned quickly answered him, 'that he took his own life. He put a rope around his neck and jumped off that big ladder as is kept for changing the bell ropes, and stuff. Ripped his head clean off. John Slane found it under a pew seven rows back. Must have rolled quite a way... damn it, Thomas, all this running to carry news gives a man a fearsome thirst!'

Taking the hint, Handiwell began to move around behind the counter, his brain already busy trying to assimilate this latest news and the impact, if any, it

20

might have on their own problems. One of the troopers had ridden off back to Portsmouth carrying a despatch from Captain Hart to Colonel Brotherwood outlining the situation and requesting additional troopers, as well as a magistrate to sign a warrant so a proper investigation of the Grayling estate could be carried out. In theory, at least, this should not be affected by the death of one fairly unimportant country minister.

However, Thomas knew only too well that things never went as smoothly as they might in a perfect world, and here in the countryside the mere fact of a good milker suddenly going dry could start tongues wagging with allegations of anything from witchcraft to the coming of the Day of Judgement.

A priest with his head ripped off in his own church.

Was there any connection with the Grayling situation? Thomas shook his head as he turned to place a generous measure of dark rum in front of Ned. It wasn't likely, at least not a direct connection. But then there was this fellow Crawley who had seized young Matilda Pennywise and turned half the village on its head. Thomas had not been present to witness the spectacle himself, but apparently the men folk had gathered like hungry wolves to watch the poor wench being scourged.

The inside of the barn, Kitty quickly saw, had been divided up into several separate sections, each one leading off a main passageway running the entire length of the near side of the building. The doors to three of these sections were closed, and whether or not they were occupied was impossible to tell. Certainly no noises came from within any of the rooms; the only sound was that of the birds in the trees outside muffled by the timber walls.

Ross thrust both girls ahead of him down the corridor until they reached the final door, which stood wide open. The light was less bright inside, coming from a series of narrow slits set high beneath the eaves, so Kitty was able to navigate around the various obstacles that sat in the centre of the enclosed space. Peering out through the eye slits in her hood, she tried to determine what these various contraptions were, but the shadows, combined with the intricacy of their construction, made this all but impossible. She could be sure of only one thing: whatever their purpose was, none of these structures had been designed with her comfort in mind.

'Get yourselves over to the end,' Ross snapped. 'Up on those benches, both of you, and be quick about it.'

As the two women stumbled forward, Kitty's eyes made out that the end wall had been divided into four sections, each of which boasted a wide bench set a couple of feet off the ground in the manner, she imagined, of bunk beds aboard ships. At either end of each bunk a chain dangled from a sturdy looking staple that terminated in a broad leather collar from which hung a metal lock. Simple, but effective, she thought. A slave on her bunk could be tethered by the neck and left with sufficient leeway to stretch out to sleep, and maybe just enough slack in the chain to step down from the bench and make use of the iron pail that she now saw had been placed beneath each bunk.

'Home sweet home,' Ross said, chuckling, 'at least for a few days, depending on how the pair of you behave yourselves.' He reached out and brought one of the collars up to Kitty's neck, securing it over the collar already resting around her throat, and the lock clicked with a hollow finality. A moment later, Sarah had been similarly secured on the next bench, at which point Ross turned away without another word and strode back out into the corridor.

Kitty blinked, shook her head, and sat for several seconds listening to the sound of his boots retreating along the stone floor, and then silence descended once more, a silence broken only by the distant, and now almost mocking, twittering of the feathered creatures outside.

'A hunt you say, Grayling?' Sir Peregrine Wellthorne raised an eyebrow, and sniffed. 'But why waste my time here on something I can do equally well at home? In fact, and begging your pardon, but the Wellthorne hunt rides over some of the finest countryside in all England.'

'Yet perhaps it does not have such interesting quarry,' Roderick Grayling suggested. He raised the brandy bottle towards his visitor, who in turn eagerly held out his glass. 'No sir, I would not offer to waste your time on something you can do better at home. A hunt here at Grayling is like no other hunt you will ever see.'

'And this quarry you hunt? Fox? Deer? Hare?'

'Birds,' Grayling replied, his smile broadening. 'Feathered little birds of a species never seen outside this estate, at least not to my knowledge.'

'Aha, fine plump fare for the pot?'

'Fine fare indeed, though not so plump, and not for the pot, though I'd wager they'll whet your appetite for certain.'

'Ah, I think I have your gist now, sir. These birds would maybe have had their wings clipped, is that what you're saying?'

'Clipped indeed, Wellthorne, but still they make fair sport. We've kept one or two back for the purpose and my lads are quick to spot any new talent. Adam has his eye on one in particular I suspect will suit you perfectly. Plump of breast and with the look of a sporting bird, he tells me.'

Wellthorne snickered. 'Sounds fascinating. So, when does the hunt begin?'

Grayling sipped his brandy. 'What say you this afternoon, sir? It will take an hour or two for the prey to be properly prepared, and I for one hate to hunt on an empty stomach. Some cold meat first would not be amiss, I think, and then we will be all the more appreciative of the warm meat we chase afterwards!'

'Definitely not foul play?' Handiwell asked again.

Ned shook his head. 'Definitely not.' He eyed the rum bottle once more.

Thomas Handiwell sighed. Ned Blaine's seemingly unquenchable thirst made gathering information more than a little costly. 'And you say Crawley has taken charge of the church itself?'

'Aye, that he has, he's got five or six of the village men with him now, some of the worst idlers and ne'er do wells for five or six miles hereabouts, including those two lads from Dummer. Paid them, I reckon, and probably promised them more. They've locked off the church completely.'

'Well, they won't be able to keep it closed off for ever,' Thomas pointed out.

Ned seized the proffered rum with ill-concealed eagerness.

'Someone will have to ride and tell the constable. Mind you, Roderick Grayling should also be told. Whilst the earl is away, his son is acting magistrate, I believe.'

'Crawley is saying it's no business of anyone save the church. Reckons he's sent a messenger to the bishop and that's an end of it. There's to be a funeral late this afternoon.'

'And what about the girl, Matilda? Word is the rogue was intending to hang her.'

'People are saying she's still going to swing, but Crawley has postponed the event out of respect to Wickstanner. Mind you, he ain't intending to put it off for long, by all accounts. Word is she's in for it tonight at sunset after the burial. Someone ought to do something about that, I reckon.' He eyed Thomas meaningfully.

The innkeeper knew that *someone* meant himself, possibly the only man in the village, besides the miller or the blacksmith, whose word carried any weight. However, as in most things, the church or its emissaries - even one whose credentials were as dubious as Crawley's - still carried the most weight of all, and there were also those in the village and its surrounds who would welcome a public execution as free entertainment. 'Maybe the blackguard will accept an appeasement,' he said finally. 'These bastards are usually as interested in gold as they are in spreading or protecting the word of the Lord, if not more so. Go down to the church, Ned, there's a good fellow, and see if you can speak with this Crawley. Tell him I'd be prepared to offer a reasonable sum for his efforts to save the girl's immortal soul so long as her earthly body is spared. I'm sure you can word it so the thieving crow understands what it is I'm saying.'

'Aye, that I can,' Ned replied. He eyed his cup, which had been emptied the moment Handiwell passed it to him.

Thomas grinned, and the grin turned to a grimace. 'When you get back, Ned,' he said firmly. 'Deliver the message and bring back a suitable answer, and there'll be a couple more of those for you.'

Ross returned only a short while later, and to Kitty's surprise his usually bland demeanour had vanished during his absence. Indeed, he looked positively angry, and she wondered who might have upset him. When he strode straight over to her she feared the worst, but if he had been tempted to take his mood out on her there was obviously someone with a greater right to her presence.

'Get outside and go with Nathan,' he snapped. 'Make sure you behave yourself, too, or when you finally come back here I'll have you perched on the thickest rogering pole there is, and you'll spend three days on it with thrashings every hour.'

Out in the corridor, the dark-haired Nathan was waiting for her. Without speaking, he hooked a leash onto Kitty's collar and gave it a sharp tug before turning away and heading towards the outer door. Helpless to do anything else, Kitty stumbled dutifully in his wake, part of her glad to leave Ross's sinister barn behind her, if only for the moment, and part of her wondering what other new tribulations lay in store for her now.

Ten minutes after leaving the barn, they came upon another one of similar size and construction, but this one was much nearer to the main barn and to the house and set in a broad clearing surrounded by trees. This building was also different in that the windows along the eaves were deeper, thus the light inside was much brighter.

'Now,' Nathan spoke for the first time as he hustled Kitty into one of the interior chambers, 'I'm going to release your hands and take this harness off you, but don't go getting any ideas. No matter how fast you think you can run, I can run a deal faster, and besides, there's nowhere much to run to. This part of the estate is well fenced, with a palisade a good ten feet high running through the woods, so I might not even chase you, but just leave you out there to wander around until you're starving fit to drop. And then, once we get you back here... well, I doubt I need tell you what you could expect.'

Glumly, Kitty shook her head.

'Right then, let's get this lot off you and get you ready for this afternoon, shall we?'

It took but a minute or two before Kitty stood completely naked. She stretched and exercised her jaw, thankful to be rid of the wadded gag, even though she suspected it was only for a short time, and although she could now once again speak, she had learned enough in her short time here to know that to do so without being bidden was most likely to earn her a swift and painful chastisement.

'Now,' Nathan said, walking across to a long bench lining the entire length of one wall, 'I'd better explain, otherwise you'll likely make a pig's ear out of the whole thing and his lordship won't be best pleased with either of us. This,' he continued, holding up what Kitty at first thought was a dead bird of astonishing proportions, 'is what you'll be wearing. You're going to be a bird,' he added, seeing the confusion on her face. 'You'll have wings, feathers and a beak and everything except, of course, you won't be able to fly. I suppose you can run?'

'Yes... yes, master,' she stammered.

'Good,' Nathan nodded, 'because this time the faster you run and the longer you run, the better the sport. You'll have the run of all the woods and the meadows within the fenced off area. It's a big area, so you can keep going quite a ways before you hit the fences, and Sir Roderick and his guests will be trying to find you. You can hide if you want, but as you can see, this plumage is very bright and deliberately so. You'll stand out pretty well and it'll take some dense undergrowth before you'll have much of a chance at staying hidden, so your best bet is to keep on the move. Understand?'

'Yes, master.' Kitty swallowed before repeating, 'Master?'

'Yes?'

'What happens if they don't catch me?'

'Oh, they'll catch you all right. There's all manner of bird traps out there, so I wouldn't worry your head about not being caught.'

'Then what happens when they do catch me?'

Nathan snorted. 'Same as happens with most birds.' He leered at her. 'You get stuffed, my girl, stuffed until you're fit to burst, or until whoever catches you loses interest or strength, and then you'll like as not be shared around. Those tits are enough to satisfy a good few appetites!'

Left alone on her bunk as Ross followed Kitty from the room, Sarah began staring about her for the first time. She saw that the centre part of the room was occupied by three timber and metal structures that had the appearance of frames, with various 'limbs' projecting at different angles. Judging by the assortment of straps hanging from different parts of these 'limbs', she realised these devices had been designed to secure people in some way or another, and that her presence here meant she would soon be strapped to one of them, at which point their exact function would be revealed to her in a manner that would leave little room for doubt or confusion.

It was not long before Ross returned and Sarah knew her latest ordeal was about to begin, for he now wore a tightly fitted pair of leather breeches, leather riding boots, and apart from thick leather bands about his wrists and throat, he was naked from the waist up.

'This is the first chamber, Sarah,' he said, speaking with surprising softness. 'What you meet in this room, what you discover about yourself, this will be as nothing compared to what awaits you further along the passage. By the time you leave here, if you ever *do* leave here, you will be a completely different person; the old you will no longer exist. Now, come forward.' He reached up, unclipped the leather collar from about her throat, and held out his arms to steady her as she swung her legs down to the floor. 'First, we shall try what I call the Princess Throne.' He guided her past the nearest structure to a most peculiar looking contraption occupying the middle of the room.

Blinking, Sarah saw its heart was a kind of seat; it looked like a wooden chair from which the first several inches had been sawn off. Furthermore, from the centre of what was left of it rose a highly polished dark wooden rod, perhaps four or five inches in length and possibly a little narrower in diameter than the flesh-and-blood counterpart she could now see bulging beneath the tight leather of Ross's breeches.

'Turn around, slave girl,' he whispered as she came to the front of the seat, and as she turned beneath his guiding hands to face away from it, she realised it was quite high for a chair, as high as the mid point of her thighs and maybe even an inch or so higher. Holding her shoulders firmly, Ross guided her backwards. 'Now open your legs wide and I'll help you sit on your throne, slave princess.' He chuckled.

Behind the mask Sarah's eyes widened in horror, for she knew there was no way she could sit upon the chair without the gleaming wooden phallus penetrating her most intimately. But as Ross continued to guide her, she understood it was to be even worse than that, for it was now apparent that it was not her vagina the rod was intended for but her one remaining virginal, and very much smaller, orifice.

'Relax, slave,' he whispered, feeling her tensing beneath his fingers. 'The little beast is well oiled and it will not stretch you that much. Come now, don't struggle against me, else I'll string you up and take a real whip to you and then make you sit on a cock twice the size of this wee thing.'

'We cannot just skulk around here and let things take their course,' James Calthorpe insisted. 'That madman could kill poor Matilda at any moment, and us none the wiser.'

'He'll not kill her yet,' Hannah Pennywise stated with an air of conviction James found quite strange. They had returned to her cottage, where she bolted the heavy door, and now she kept scurrying across to the window and peering down the lane that led to the village. 'He'll want to use her first, and not in that way, although I fear that's already been done to the poor lass. No, young James, Crawley has a readymade scapegoat in his hands helpless as you like. Yon fool vicar-man's death will be laid fair and square at her feet though we both know she had nothing to do with it, save it appears he may well have regretted himself and not been able to live with the shame of his doings. Aye, Crawley will guess as much too, and he'll want to make sure he gets his corn from it.'

'But he can only hang her once, can't he?' James pointed out.

Hannah sighed. 'Aye, that he can,' she said, 'but all the time he keeps her alive... well, she's worth more to him alive than dead, at least for the moment. If he paints her so that folk believe she can witch a priest into jumping off a ladder with a hemp rope round his throat, there's some who'll believe she'd be capable of anything and would pay the one remaining church fellow to make sure her powers can't reach them from beyond the grave.'

'I don't understand,' James said. 'You mean Crawley will demand payments from the villagers in return for some spurious promise that he can protect them against whatever powers Matilda is supposed to possess?'

Hannah nodded. 'You understand well enough. If that's not exactly what I think he'll do, it'll be something not that far different. I once watched a man not unlike Jacob Crawley do exactly that, and not just that one time either. All over several counties he worked his evil, though I only saw him the once in a village in Kent where a cousin of mine lived. It was a few years back now, maybe as many as a score, but the fellow's methods were just the same, and the simple country fools were in more terror of him come the end than they were of the so-

26

called witches he went around stringing up everywhere.'

'Matthew Hopkins,' James whispered to himself.

'That'd be the one, the black-hearted carrion bastard! But how do you know of him? You'd have been no more than a wee sprig of a thing when last he was heard of.'

'Book learning, mistress,' James replied. 'Matthew Hopkins and accounts of his doings appear in several texts, but I had supposed the sort of superstitions he manipulated had long since died out.'

'Believe that if you like,' Hannah snarled, 'but then you just go back down to the village and take a look around at the faces and the eyes of the people. Fear lurks never far behind superstition and ignorance, and those two venomous fiends are never far beneath the surface, whatever polish people might put on it.'

'Some of us know better,' James protested. 'My father, Master Handiwell from the inn, Mistress Merridew and John Slane the smithy, to name but less than a handful, and if we all band together and speak out against this lunacy, people will have to listen. We are all respected people around here, even myself despite my lack of years. And then there's Sir Roderick. If I ride to the Hall and put the facts before him, then he must surely be forced to intervene, for when news of this reaches London there will be questions asked if he sits back and does nothing.'

'Questions, maybe,' Hannah retorted sourly, 'but I've yet to see a Grayling who worried enough to ever give an answer worth a penny. Grayling might intervene, but if he does so, it'll be for his own purposes, and I'd not trust that young whelp a foot further than I could throw him. There are things going on out there I wouldn't want to look too closely at, for I'd not like Roderick Grayling to suspect I knew even the first thing of his private business, not if I expected to live to see the end of the week!'

Kitty stared down at herself as Nathan continued tightening the laces at her back. The garment was made of soft leather like a jerkin that extended down to her lower stomach in a V-shape, though with two circular openings cut into its front through which her breasts protruded prominently from among the thick covering of feathers that had been stitched to the leather. The same feathered covering stretched down the leather sleeves into which her arms and hands had been pushed, the sleeves laced tightly so that the elbows were all but inflexible, and the fingers and thumbs held firm and flat in pointed mitten endings. Thin strips of metal had also been stitched to these sleeves, with more leather stretched between them and still more feathers stitched to this. It had taken someone a long time to make this bizarre garment, Kitty reflected, but it had also taken a very peculiar mind to envisage a design which, now that it was in place, gave her arms the appearance of wings while at the same time rendering them, and her hands, all but useless.

Nathan had laced up as far as the base of her neck and here he paused, stepping back and walking slowly around her to examine the effect. Apparently, he found it to his satisfaction for he smiled broadly and nodded. 'Very good,' he said, reaching out a hand to tug at one of her nipple rings.

Kitty flinched, but made no attempt to pull back.

'Plump breasts, and we'll make them plumper still, but first we need to get the head on you.'

The bird head was in fact a hood almost identical to the one Kitty had been wearing throughout most of her captivity, except that stiffened leather had been stitched over the outside of the mouth and shaped to form a beak which had either been dyed or painted a bright yellow. A big crest of blue, red and yellow feathers ran over the crown of her head from front to back, with more feathers shorter than those of the crest covering most of the rest of the hood, the neck of which, once it was laced closed, was intended to sit inside the neck of the jerkin Nathan now proceeded to lace higher still.

The effect of the two tightly laced necklines was that Kitty found she could now barely bend her head, and sideways movement was also severely restricted. And to make matters worse, the eye slits were surrounded on their outer edge by two small curved pieces of leather that projected outward, limiting her field of vision to a narrow arc enabling her only to see straight ahead.

'Now for these bubbies.' Smiling, Nathan moved around in front of her, and carefully moving the plumage aside began to pull on laces that ran through the soft leather at the base of her bosom. As the openings began to constrict, Kitty felt her breasts begin to bulge out and distend, and the pressure quickly caused a reaction in her nipples, which became even more engorged and prominent than usual. 'Now there's a bird fit for stuffing if ever there was one,' he declared.

Kitty bit into the fresh leather wadding between her teeth and stared mutely back at him, wondering if he intended to sample the bird before whatever was to come.

Nathan, however, was not yet finished with her costume. 'These boots,' he said, taking up the first one, 'have iron plates in the soles, so you'll find them a bit heavy, but that's the point; don't want you able to run forever, else the guests are likely to become bored. You'll also be thankful for them because at least they'll protect your feet and legs from stones and most of the brambles.'

Each boot was long, reaching halfway between Kitty's knee and crotch, and as she shuffled the first shod foot experimentally, she certainly felt the weight. She also felt her leg muscles being constricted as Nathan set about tightening the laces, and wondered if the footwear had been made with a far more slender girl in mind. But as she stood peering down between the twin mounds of her bulging breasts, she guessed the tight fit was deliberate, for her legs, sheathed now for the most part in gleaming brown leather, had taken on an altogether different shape from the one she was used to seeing.

While Kitty was musing on her transformation, Nathan once more returned to the bench and took up a short, tapering strap she saw was attached to a set of extraordinarily long feathers. On the other side of the strap, she also glimpsed two stubby protrusions of gleaming black leather, the one slightly longer and a good deal thicker than the other. Instinctively she tried to draw back, immediately understanding where these twin phallus objects were designed to go.

Her captor leapt forward and grasped her fiercely by the shoulder. 'Don't be a stupid little slut!' he hissed. 'This is your tail, and you're going to end up wearing it one way or another, so why not save me a lot of bother and yourself a good whipping? If I send you out to the hunt with a red arse, it ain't going to make a whit of difference to anyone, saving you, of course!'

Kitty's shoulders slumped and she felt as if at least half her strength had drained out of her body. He was right, of course. Resistance was futile. She would not leave the barn without the two dildos inside her, and the gorgeous tail plumage bobbing behind her. With a low whimper of surrender, she slowly moved her legs apart.

The two leather shafts had been pre-oiled and slipped into her easily enough, although the introduction of the rear one to her bottom hole initially caused an involuntary contraction of her sphincter muscles, so that she had to make a conscious effort to relax them. That done, it slid in with surprising ease. As Nathan finished buckling the strap that held them in place and supported her tail, she began to experience a peculiar feeling of warmth and fullness, and when she took her first step, a mere half pace to keep her balance, the feeling intensified tenfold.

'Well, there we are.' He took several steps back and tilted his head from side to side, stepping this way and that and bidding her turn around slowly and display her tail feathers. 'Yes, very pretty indeed, Titty Kitty, but then you're not Titty Kitty any more, at least not for this afternoon. Now you're what his lordship calls a fucky-fucky bird, and by the heavens, come midnight, you'll most certainly have been fucky-fucked to a turn!'

'So, what exactly are we supposed to be looking for, Paddy?' Trooper Sean Kelly leaned against his musket and yawned.

Sergeant Paddy Riley scratched the side of his nose. 'To be honest with you, Sean, I'm not rightly knowing, not exactly, anyway. But a couple of ladies being held against their will would be as likely a starting place as any, and meantime, if we do have to knock over a couple of those murdering bastards, I'll not be losing too much sleep over it.'

'Well, they shot Hollis without even giving a warning. I'll not be having any doubts about what needs doing. Only thing that worries me, though,' Kelly continued thoughtfully, 'is that this place belongs to some earl, and us just a couple of humble troopers.'

'Humble or not, we're following a direct order from an officer, and it'll be his head on the block if there's trouble. We just make sure we keep our hides in one piece, and *his*,' Riley added, jerking a thumb at Toby Blaine, who was standing quietly by the side of the lane, head cocked to one side as if listening for something.

'Yeah, well, I'm not sure it's such a good idea to have the lad along,' Kelly muttered. 'He's not much more than a babe. Look at him, will you!'

'I've had troopers only a few months older than him,' Riley said blandly. 'The lad knows the lie of the land hereabouts, which we two don't. Isn't that so, young Toby?'

Without turning to look at them, Toby nodded. 'I know most of it, Mister Riley,' he confirmed, 'but not right into the estate. There's areas that are fenced off and patrolled by keepers all the time, so we never push our luck, not when there's rabbits enough elsewhere.'

'Sensible lad,' Riley grinned. 'Never go further than the pot's needs, that's what my da' used to say, probably still saying it, the old bastard. And yes, Sean Kelly,' he grinned fiercely at the trooper, 'I not only *have* a da', he actually did marry me ma and I do know him, contrary to certain stories going the company rounds.'

'Sure, and I know that, sergeant darling,' Kelly smirked, 'and didn't I grow up only a spit and a toss down the road from you anyway?'

'And probably listened to a few rumours there, too.' Riley shook his head as he turned back to Toby. 'Well then, lad, it's time we started on the serious stuff. We're relying on you to be a good scout and keep us out of trouble as far as possible. Reckon you can do that?'

'I'll try my best, sir,' Toby replied. 'And if Mistress Harriet is in there somewhere, I'd recognise her a half mile off, don't you worry none about that.'

Aye, Riley thought, *and you're as sweet on the lady as a puppy for a lamb bone.* As they moved off single file into the trees, he tried to prevent his mind from straying back to thoughts of another young boy, and a certain married farmer's daughter in Kerry County.

Sarah felt as if she had been stuffed close to the bursting point so the slightest motion sent searing spasms she could not identify coursing through her body. She scarcely dared move a muscle as she sat perched on the edge of the seat, and she made no effort to resist when Ross took each of her arms in turn and drew it out to secure it at the wrist to the horizontal beam that ran at shoulder height behind her. Once the wrist straps had been tightly buckled, another was passed about her throat and yet another about her waist so that, from the seat up, she was now held completely immobile. Beneath the seat two more beams projected out at angles just above the ground, and to the ends of these Ross shackled her ankles so her feet no longer touched the packed earth and her legs were drawn apart to lewdly display her naked and shaven sex.

Sarah made a futile effort to close her thighs, but even though she was still able to move her knees, doing so placed a terrible strain on her muscles and she quickly abandoned the effort. Blinking through the eye slits, she watched Ross where he stood before her, his face impassive save for a slight flicker of feeling in his eyes.

'How does your new throne feel now, princess?' he asked softly. 'I must say, you suit it beautifully, and now you must enjoy it for a while.' He started to turn away. 'I'm afraid I don't have any subjects for you just now, my lady,' he said mockingly, 'but I shall undoubtedly return to pay homage to your true crown before nightfall. Meantime, I shall leave you alone to enjoy some royal thoughts.'

At first Kitty found the heavy-soled boots most awkward, but as she moved along down the path ahead of Nathan, she discovered herself growing accustomed to their weight and the unusual angle at which they held her feet, so that she was soon moving with surprising ease and knew she would be able to run when the time came. How long she would be able to keep going, however, was a different matter altogether and she did not doubt Nathan's assertion that eventual capture was inevitable. She began to wonder if it was worth making any real effort to run in the first place, but as if reading her mind, Nathan quickly banished the thought.

'Fucky-fucky birds that are caught too quickly end up getting a special basting for the table,' he informed her. 'I've seen sluggish girls with their entire bodies looking like they've been baked in an oven for a couple of hours, with not a pink stripe between all the red ones. They never get caught quickly a second time.'

The hunt was scheduled to start from behind the house itself, a huge, two-winged building of dark stone with what appeared to be a recently added third wing of red brick jutting out at a most peculiar angle. The original structure formed a perimeter on three sides of an expansive lawn that was bounded on the fourth side by well-kept flowerbeds. Behind them were more tall grasses, bushes and trees that grew closer and closer together the further away from the house they went until eventually they merged with the main woodland.

As Nathan prodded her forward across the grass, Sarah saw that she was not the only quarry of the day: four more equally bizarre birdlike creatures stood in a group watched over by two liveried footmen, while a fifth female crouched on all fours, her features, except for her mouth and lower jaw, hidden beneath a wolverine mask, her entire body, save for her breasts, buttocks and crotch, swathed in a skin-tight suit of short fur. Kitty saw that where the fur did not cover her, the girl's flesh was a musky brown colour, and guessed she was probably of foreign origin, although not as dark as the African slaves she had seen in the past few months.

'That's Oona,' Nathan told her, noting her interest even though Kitty had tried to conceal it. 'Comes from the Indies and she's one of the master's favourites. She's a good hunting bitch, and they reckon she can sniff a warm pussy at two hundred paces if the wind's blowing in the right direction. If she catches you first, those teeth will make yours sing, believe me. You'll be glad of the cunt strap then, and you'd better pray the hunters come up before Oona gets it off you.'

31

Kitty felt herself turn cold as she stared at the wolf-girl. Oona, seeing the newcomer, looked up and bared her teeth, her long tongue lolling out of her mouth in a doglike fashion. Kitty bit into her gag and barely managed to stifle a whimper of terror as she turned her head away to avoid the piercing, primitive stare with which the girl seemed determined to pin her. If anything could encourage Kitty to run, and keep on running until the last dregs of strength drained from her legs, it would be the memory of those eyes and teeth.

When the shadowy figures first burst into the crypt and began stripping her bondage from her, Matilda Pennywise felt a surge of relief course through her body, but her rising spirits were just as swiftly dashed on rocks of despair as she realised she was simply exchanging one captivity for another. And this one, even though the threat of imminent death had apparently been removed for the moment, was in many ways more frightening, and certainly more bewildering than what she had experienced at the hands of Crawley and his minions.

As she stood beside the other bird-girls now, despite the warmth of the steadily climbing sun she felt herself shivering with trepidation. She wondered what it was she had done to offend her Maker that he had thrown her into yet another pit of depravity and terror. At first she assumed these people must have something to do with that awful witchfinder, but as she listened to snatches of conversation, she came to understand that her new captors were something else entirely. Furthermore, as the women unmasked once they were away from the village, Matilda had been astonished to recognise one of them as Jane Handiwell, the innkeeper's daughter, and yet another as Lady Ellen Grayling, the daughter of the earl and younger sister of Sir Roderick.

Both physically and mentally exhausted from her ordeal at Crawley's hands, it took Matilda some time to realise the full import of her new situation. She had never seen Grayling Hall close up before, but she had glimpsed it several times from the hill across the wide valley, so she recognised its outlines. Looking about her now, she began to understand just why the Graylings kept the place so well guarded. This was a different world altogether, and a world no normal person would ever believe existed. Where Crawley's wickedness was based on a brutal greed, this was a reality founded upon lust alone, or so it seemed. It was a place where human beings were reduced to the status of animals, or even worse to helpless playthings for the amusement and satisfaction of people to whom morality was an alien concept. Their attitude towards their captives was impossible to describe. Matilda knew that not one of the men she had met so far had the slightest interest in her as a person. All she was to them was an object, a creature, a *fucky-fucky* bird as the fellow had called her when he forced the leather plug into her bottom and tightened the strap from which her long tail now sprang. She was a creature to be harried and hunted, and after that... she shuddered again, more violently than before, and fought against the salty tears springing into her hooded eyes.

Harriet recognised all the men who came to her in turn and used her helpless body like slavering beasts, clearly unable to believe their good fortune, and just as obviously not giving a single thought to the poor girl inside the mask. The fact that they assumed she was Matilda did nothing to lessen her ordeal; if anything, it served to emphasise the cruelty of her tormentors, for she doubted they would have worried who it was Crawley had turned over to them, and even if they suspected her true identity it would have made little or no difference to them.

In her eyes, the five men who took her represented the worst element of their little local society, although only one of them, Peter Farren, actually lived in the village itself. In theory, he was a wheelwright, but he had not worked much in that trade since old John Tyler the wagon maker died and his daughter passed the business on to a cousin in a village five miles to the south. Every week or so, Farren would ride down and work for a day or two, but in between he barely earned a living labouring on the surrounding farms. His reputation as a drinker and a sloth meant that even this work was sparse as he was only ever hired during the busiest parts of the season.

The same was more or less true of the other four. One, George Prentice, was the youngest son of a sheep farmer. He scrounged enough from the old man to drink and gamble, and did only as much as was necessary to persuade Harry Prentice not to kick him out. Alfred Diggins went from village to village and from farm to farm performing odd repair jobs and ditch clearing. His brother, Edward helped him occasionally and from time to time went off to the city for unspecified reasons.

The fifth man was originally a Londoner, Thaddeus Gilbert. What he did for a living no one really knew for he was never seen to work locally. It was rumoured he had originally been a thief in the capital and that he kept a hoard of gold coins hidden somewhere around the small cottage he rented from James Calthorpe's father, the miller Francis Calthorpe. Like the others, he spent much of his time in the *Black Drum*, but unlike them he never seemed short of a shilling or two, and would stand his drinking cronies rounds when they were short of cash.

Jacob Crawley would not have had to offer this seedy band much by way of inducement to join him, Harriet reflected grimly. There was not one among them who might not have sold his own grandmother if the price was right, and they would see acting as the witchfinder's bodyguard an easy way to make extra drinking money.

Harriet blinked, and looked up as yet another shadow loomed over her. It was Thaddeus Gilbert again, the third time he had come to her in what was probably no more than two hours, although time was now something Harriet had no way of judging accurately. He stood over her, unbuckled his belt and dropped his breeches, revealing the massive penis she now knew only too well.

'Get your legs open, slut,' he commanded in a raspy voice without further ceremony. 'Can't waste a good pussy while it's still available. Mind you, if your grandmamma comes up with the money, we might get to enjoy each other's company for a day or so longer, eh? I hope she does, sister, for both our sakes. I seen too many pretty wenches dancing on the end of the rope to find the prospect as good as the alternative. Now lay ye back, and try to act like you're alive this time, otherwise I'll like as not take my belt to your arse!'

Sarah was almost relieved when Ross returned, even though she knew what must inevitably follow. How long she had remained spread-eagled and impaled upon that terrible seat she could not tell, but the sound of the blood pulsing in her temples seemed to have grown both louder and slower, and her shadowy prison felt as if it had slipped into a timeless eternity of its own.

'Still comfortable on the throne, I see,' Ross remarked dryly.

Sarah peered out at him wondering just what sort of man could treat a fellow human in this fashion, and apparently even find humour in her plight. Had she not been gagged so efficiently, she knew she would have felt compelled to launch upon him a stream of invectives that would have had both her parents turning in their graves. As it was, all she could do was sit and glare back at him.

'By the time you leave here,' Ross said, moving closer to her, 'you'll think nothing of opening your legs to any man that commands you.' He reached out and with the backs of two fingers traced a feathery line down the length of her gaping sex lips.

Before she could stop herself, Sarah felt a tremble of spiky heat run from her groin up her spine and explode inside her head like a small fireball.

'You see,' Ross said, smiling thinly, 'there are already some things you cannot keep yourself from doing and being. You're beginning to understand that you no longer have any control over your existence, nor any control over the way in which your body wants to react. Quite soon now your flesh will demand things that only a short time ago you would surely have found abhorrent in the extreme, and you will crawl willingly at the feet of any master who you think might give them to you.' He reached out and gently ran one fingertip about her right nipple.

Again a shiver passed up her back.

'Not so big as Titty Kitty, but pretty titties all the same.' He moved his finger to her left nipple.

Although Sarah tried to steel herself, the resulting sensation was almost identical.

'If I'd done that to you in a drawing room a day or so ago,' Ross drawled, 'I daresay you'd have slapped my face and cried out for your servants to toss me into the street, but already you're understanding that feeling of helplessness a slave needs to experience as her entire life. Do you feel yourself to be a slave yet? Hmm, maybe not quite yet, but very soon I promise you will.' His fingers descended to her labia again, and this time probed just between them.

To Sarah's horror, she realised she was quite wet down there as the two digits slipped easily over her lubricated flesh.

34

Ross chuckled, and probed slightly deeper. 'Your body understands what your mind is still fighting against,' he told her. 'Here you are, primed and ready for a hot cock, and yet inside your head you still want to fight it, to fight even the desire for one. Shall I put my hot cock in here for your body's sake, slave Sarah?' Abruptly he stepped back, breaking the intimate contact. 'Maybe not just yet,' he said teasingly. 'Maybe we should encourage your body with a few more little tricks.' He leaned forward, and suddenly his lips were around her left nipple. He sucked on it, drawing it into his mouth until the ring beneath it was pressed against his lower lip.

Sarah groaned into her gag and only the broad strap about her waist prevented her from arching forward with an instinct she would never have believed herself capable of.

'Very nice,' Ross commented, straightening up and stepping back again. 'Let's try the other one.' Leaning forward again, he repeated the action on her other nipple.

This time Sarah was ready for the shockwaves, yet still she could do no more than fight the urge to jerk forward against the straps, for her head quickly began to buzz and she could feel the first warm trickle of her escaping juices on her inner thighs.

'Now your body is really betraying you,' Ross informed her. 'We both know I could take you easily now. If I removed your gag, would you perhaps even beg me to take you? No, I think not.' He shook his head. 'Your mind would still make you cry out and curse me, no doubt, whatever your body really wanted. And that's what this is all about, slave girl, freeing you from the mental restraints of years with the physical restraints in which you now sit. But be assured, my sweet little cock-sheath, free you I shall, and quicker than you might think!'

They came to the fence about a mile-and-a half into the woods. It was a simple structure, with eight or nine inch square sectioned posts driven deep into the ground every fifteen paces or so, and horizontal lengths fixed a few inches above the ground a similar distance from the top. To these had been nailed thinner vertical palings, set four or five inches apart, forming an impenetrable barrier some ten feet high and offering no purchase for a would be climber.

'They must have cut down half these woods to build this,' Paddy Riley whispered, grinning at his two companions. He looked to left and right, to where the fence disappeared as far as the eye could see along the broad swathe cut through trees in either direction, a further precaution against anyone using nature as an aid to scaling the perimeter. 'You say this goes all the way round? How far, for the love of Michael?'

'Miles,' Toby grinned back. 'But they didn't get all this timber from the woods here,' he added. 'I remember when I was young there were wagons coming and going for weeks, and all these men down from London, most of them. Spent nigh on the entire summer putting this lot up.'

'Like their privacy, for sure,' Sean Kelly observed dryly. He peered up at the sharpened tops of the palings. 'Are we going over or under, me old sergeant friend? I've got a length of rope in me pack and a small trencher, too. The earth here feels a bit hard though, and I reckon they'll have bedded these bastards in a good foot or so.'

'We'll go through,' Paddy said. 'I've a small saw here, not nearly so big as I'd like, so it'll take maybe half an hour, but I'd rather take the time and make sure we have a decent bolthole if we get rumbled. A man trying to shin up over this lot would make a good target for those bastards, and we've already seen how straight they can shoot.'

'What about the dogs?' Toby reminded him. 'They've got keepers with dogs patrolling, and those dogs hear just about anything louder than a rabbit farting.'

'We'll just have to go real slow like,' Paddy said. He heaved the pack off his shoulder and dropped it to the ground at his feet. A moment later he was drawing out a foot long blade with a gleaming, serrated edge. 'My da' used to use this to cut into Lord Fleming's barns and hencoops. I nicked it off him ten years ago, and just sort of forgot to give it back. Useful little tool this is and I'm never without it. Amazing what uses something like this can have to a soldier on his travels, but then that's a whole lot of other stories and we've got work to do. Sean, you get along that way about fifty yards, and Toby, you do the same the other way. Keep your eyes peeled and your ears flapped well back and whistle to me if you hear anything. And Sean, the first sign of anyone with anything that looks like it might shoot, make sure you pick the bugger off before he gets a chance to take a pot shot in my direction. You let me catch one, and by the Holy Mother I'll come back and haunt you for sure!'

'Are these costumes entirely necessary, Grayling?' Sir Peregrine Wellthorne peered down at himself and wrinkled his nose. The tight leather breeches and figure-hugging jerkin had been dyed black to match the heavy boots. Alongside him, Roderick Grayling stood similarly dressed, except he also wore a black leather hood mask that covered his features down to just below his nose, leaving two narrow slits for his eyes.

'Not *entirely* necessary my dear fellow,' Grayling chuckled, 'but they do serve a purpose as defence against thorns and suchlike, and the masks add an element of mystery that is slightly terrifying to our quarry. Besides, this way they have little idea who it is that is actually bearing down on them, any more than we can tell one of the pretty feathered things from another.'

'Well, I must say, I feel a trifle foolish,' Peregrine complained, eyeing the mask he held in his hands with a mixture of suspicion and distaste. He looked around the drawing room as if expecting someone to burst in on them at any moment.

Grayling laid a reassuring hand on his arm. 'Relax, Wellthorne,' he urged. 'Take some more brandy and then get your mask on and no one will know who you are. There are three more guests to join the hunt, and none of them has any idea as to the identity of the others any more than you would know them or they you.'

Peregrine sniffed, and walked heavily across to the cabinet upon which the brandy decanter stood.

'Not too heavy on that,' Grayling called out. 'Not that I mind how much of my brandy you drink while you're here, for you're an honoured guest, but it helps to keep the head reasonably clear for the hunt itself. A fellow can break an ankle if he trips over a trailing root or a stray chunk of stone.'

'Tell me, Grayling,' Wellthorne replaced the decanter and picked up his glass goblet, 'these pistols we're using, you're sure they don't injure these girls permanently?'

'Of course not,' Grayling assured him, smiling. 'I'd not risk wasting valuable merchandise just for a few hours fun. No, all they fire is a soft pellet of thin leather sewn about oil-soaked muslin. They sting like hell and can knock the wind out of a girl, but they're not very accurate above twenty paces, so we have to get in fairly close, which makes it more of a sport, don't you think?'

'Seems to me a fellow would have to get very lucky, or else land several hits, in order to bring his bird to ground,' Peregrine observed.

Grayling nodded. 'The knack is to hit the right places,' he said. 'In the stomach or the lower chest will wind them for sure, and a hit around the top of the leg numbs the muscles and usually sends them into spasms, which makes running much harder. A hit on the head will usually stun them completely, but the head is off limits here. If the slug catches the wrong spot it can kill, and we did lose one girl last year. So no head shots, please. Have yourself some sport with a few shots at their titties, by all means. But remember, you want to enjoy the prize to the full afterwards, so you want to keep your bird wide awake for the table!' He turned away and walked across to the window looking out across the lawn. 'Well sir, as soon as you've finished your drink I think we should make a start. It doesn't hurt to keep the birds waiting for a little while, keeps them nicely on their toes, but time marches on and the sun is almost overhead now.'

Matilda's original fear and confusion had begun to clear and was now beginning to metamorphose into a cold determination. Peering out from her feathered bird mask, she watched as various grooms and servants moved about through a steadily growing knot of what she could tell was mostly nobility, even if some of their number were most curiously garbed themselves. To her surprise she saw there were women amongst them; women dressed in lavish silks and satins she was sure would not have been out of place in the late king's court, their hair piled high and beset with glittering jewelled pins and bright ribbons. Their painted faces were animated with an excited lust reflecting that on the features of their men folk, at least on the features not hidden behind those dreadful black masks.

One of the younger grooms had taken great delight in explaining to the bird-girls that these were the actual hunters and that the others were merely spectators, some of whom would be watching from hides and platforms set among the trees while the women would watch and wait from the lawn, eager, no doubt, to see the captured bird slaves brought home in triumph.

A red-haired female, the youngest among their number as far as Matilda could tell, kept drifting towards the bird-girls, and although she did not approach them directly, her interest was obvious. *What does she find so intriguing about a few helpless females dressed so ridiculously?* Matilda wondered. Was it their near-nakedness despite their feather coverings, or was it just their overall pitiful plight she was mocking by her nearness and the contrast with her own beautifully tailored finery compared with their gaudy feather traps?

One of the unmasked men called out to the redhead. 'I say, Isobel,' his face was flushed with drink and excitement, 'what on earth is going through that pretty head of yours? I swear, you've looked over every inch of these pretty little tweeters not once but a dozen times. Fancy someone to hunt one for you, do you?'

The young woman rounded on the fellow, eyes blazing. 'If I did,' she snapped, 'I'd not choose you as my champion, Guy Bressingham. I wouldn't trust you to sit a horse in that state, let alone try to track one of these pretties through Roderick's wood. You'd like as not fall and break your fool neck, if I know you!'

'Tish!' Bressingham chided her, raising a hand in a mock defensive gesture. 'You're too cruel my dear, too cruel by half. Give me half a good reason and I'd be as good a hunter as any you care to name, but then I don't see you as a hunted bird, more's the pity.'

'And if you did,' Isobel retorted, 'it'd take more than you've got to ruffle my feathers!'

'But we'll never know, will we?' Bressingham replied, and deliberately yawned. 'I'd wager five hundred guineas I'd have you within the hour, but then you wouldn't take that risk, would you?'

Immediately, several heads turned and even Matilda's ears pricked up. *Five hundred guineas?* That was a small fortune, even in these circles.

'Hah, a wager, is it?' another man asked. He was some years older than Bressingham and going badly to fat, which certainly precluded him from anything as active as this hunt. 'Why, I'll offer even money on Bressingham to anyone who wants to take it. I'm sorry, my dear Isobel,' he leered at her, 'but the odds are against any of these birds remaining on the loose for more than a couple of hours at best, and I doubt you'd be quite as quick as they.'

'And why do you doubt that, my lord?' Isobel snapped. 'Just because I haven't spent my life scrubbing floors and carrying buckets doesn't mean I cannot run. Besides, brains come into the equation, and I'd back my intelligence against a dozen of these silly whores.'

'Ah, so you'll accept my challenge?' Bressingham laughed, and the young redhead looked suddenly confused and alarmed. 'Or perhaps your brains aren't really what you claim them to be?' he added.

Matilda gawped in disbelief as the scene unfolded before her. Surely this young noblewoman wasn't intending to allow herself to be put through the same humiliation that had been inflicted upon herself and these other girls? And yet... maybe that was why she had been so interested in them in the first place, she reasoned. Perhaps she had been looking at them and wondering what it would feel like to be so helpless, to know that soon she must run, if not for her life then at least for her honour, whatever remained of it. Whatever the reason, the redheaded fool seemed reluctant to back down.

'If you're so certain, Bressingham,' she was saying, 'and if Lord Wormley is offering even money on you, surely you can do better with your own odds?'

'Six to four,' Wormley suggested. The knot of guests was drawing in closer now, eager to see the outcome of this contest.

Isobel looked at the paunchy lord with obvious contempt. 'Six to four?' she echoed. 'Pah! Have you no sense of chivalry? Lay me three to one and I'll maybe give it some serious consideration.'

'I'd lay her anytime,' Matilda heard one of the other men nearest to the bird-girls mutter to his companion, but he was far enough away that Isobel could not hear his jibe.

'Two to one,' Wormley offered.

'And I'll lay you five to two myself,' Bressingham announced, 'but that's a private wager between the two of us. Wormley has the rights to the main book, and I'd not presume.'

'Five hundred guineas at five to two, you say?' Isobel's eyes narrowed and the corners of her mouth twitched. 'One hour only? I stay free of you for one hour, and I wear a marking so the other hunters know I'm to be prey only to you?'

'Agreed,' Bressingham replied.

Lord Wormley nodded. 'Agreed, so long as Grayling has no objections.'

'Indeed, I haven't.' The masked figure had appeared unnoticed from a glass-panelled door opening directly onto the lawn from the library. Behind him followed a second similarly attired figure, but there was no mistaking Grayling, even beneath his disguise. 'No objections whatsoever,' he added, 'and I'll lay a hundred guineas on you myself, Isobel.'

'But she must be garbed and treated exactly as the other birds,' Bressingham insisted. 'The full costume, if you please, down to the very last detail.'

To Matilda, the two dildos inside her suddenly seemed to grow to twice their actual size and she felt a chill of incredulity course through her. Did this silly spoiled brat know exactly what she was being manoeuvred into agreeing to? Would she yet draw back from the brink, or would pride...?

'Agreed!' Isobel declared. She turned to the cluster of bird slaves. 'I'm afraid you poor things will have to wait around a little longer. Sir Roderick, I presume you have a maid who will help me prepare?'

Thomas Handiwell had said to Hart, 'I fear this will be a wasted effort,' and

39

now, as they were confronted by the grim-faced men who stood beyond the towering iron gates marking the boundary of the Grayling estate, he could see he was to be proved correct in his assumption.

At this stage the perimeter wall was built of stone and brick, a massive, impossible to scale edifice that rose maybe twenty feet on either side of the solid gateposts with their stone lions glaring down upon the road. Just within stood a small blockhouse that afforded shelter to the four men who guarded the gate, four armed men who could presumably call upon reinforcements if they thought their outpost was under serious threat. Only one of them appeared to be armed, and that with only a pistol tucked into his belt, but Handiwell felt certain there would be other weaponry at hand if required, and that they would seize it long before any serious attempt could be made to force open the heavy gates.

It was the pistol carrier who came up to the thick bars as they approached. No, he replied in response to Handiwell's opening question, Sir Roderick was not receiving visitors this day. No, he would not take a message up to the house, but if the gentlemen cared to leave a written note, he would see to it that it was passed to Sir Roderick, and he felt certain a messenger would be sent if the gentleman was prepared to grant them an interview. And no, he knew nothing about banditry, abduction, or highwaymen, and the presence of armed men elsewhere in the woods was none of his business, although he knew Sir Roderick had grown tired of poachers taking his game.

'No man goes to such length to protect a few deer and pheasants,' Handiwell muttered when they had wheeled their horses around and begun the long trot back towards the main road. 'And Grayling must have something akin to a small army in there.'

'I'd say he has quite a private force,' Hart agreed. 'Certainly my small band would appear to be heavily outnumbered, and even if they do agree to send more men up from Portsmouth, well, if Grayling has a mind, it would take quite a battle to force a way in there.'

'I think Riley had it right, though the cheek of the Irish blackguard annoys me at times. A full frontal assault is not the way, at least not at this time. Without proof that it was Grayling's men shooting at us then the fellow is quite within his rights to protect his own property, and I cannot see any magistrate granting us a warrant.'

'Then we must pray that your two Irishmen succeed where we cannot,' Handiwell said, 'though it pains me to think we must trust all to a couple of ex-poachers and a young boy who'll probably end up in the colonies, or swinging from a rope for poaching himself!'

Ross seemed totally unhurried and completely unworried by Sarah's obvious discomfort. He drew a pipe from a pocket in his jacket that he filled with deliberate precision and then lit, walking about the chamber puffing deeply and filling the air with acrid tobacco fumes. At first Sarah tried to follow him with her eyes, but she soon gave up on this and returned to staring directly in front of her, trying to ignore the persistent pressure of the leather-covered shaft upon which she sat, and the dull throbbing now emanating from her groin.

'A shame they needed Titty Kitty for other sport,' he mused as he stepped back into her line of sight. 'She's got a hungry little mouth and an active tongue I should have liked to see lapping away at your pussy for a while. Well, maybe tomorrow. I doubt she'll be available before that, unless she's caught by that old fellow from Plymouth who looks as if just the hunt would cripple him, let alone a good fuck afterwards.

'Now then,' he went on, lowering the pipe and staring straight at her, 'I think maybe we should do something for those pretty bubbies. I have just the thing here somewhere, if you'll excuse me for a moment. Don't you go away.' Laughing to himself, he moved across to the bench where Sarah heard him rummaging through its contents, until a soft exclamation indicated he had found whatever it was he was looking for. It turned out to be what she recognised from illustrations as a cat-o'-nine-tails, although it seemed much smaller than she had imagined, and the leather thongs looked much shorter and lighter.

Ross brandished it before her, smiling. 'This is what we call a *tit whip*, slave. A fraction the size of the real thing - though we do use the real thing on a girl's tits if she deserves it, so I should make sure I behaved myself if I were you - and just right for a pair of lovely bubbies like yours. See?' He flicked his wrist and sent the tendrils snaking across Sarah's right breast.

The thongs barely made a sound as they fell across her taut flesh, but a wave of fire shot through her that made her writhe against her bondage as the painful heat seared her entire being. Another flick of his wrist, and this time the whip fell across her left breast, at least two of the leather strands catching her nipple and causing an explosive sensation that was at once pain and desire.

'I can see my little toy is going to have exactly the desired effect today,' he said, and flicked his wrist two times in succession.

Despite the gag, Sarah heard a plaintive mewling gurgle she knew could only have come from her own throat. She knew also, as the fire began rising inside her, that if it were not for the gag she would surely cry out for him to stop this new torture and fill her instead with the weapon she could see bulging against his tight leather breeches. *Anything*, she thought wildly as she closed her eyes and wriggled and gasped beneath the next pair of assaults, *anything* had to be better than enduring this unfulfilled agony much longer!

And then it seemed that even Ross realised she could take no more, that she was hovering over a precipice whose brink, once crossed, might mean the end of her very sanity, because the steady whipping stopped.

She opened her eyes, and as she tried to focus, she saw that he was already standing naked before her, poised between her widespread knees, his manhood rearing up as eager for her as she was for it. She felt his hard smoothness pressing against a portal already wide open and inviting, its wet lips offering no resistance to entry. Indeed, her inner tunnel seemed to reach out and draw the throbbing phallus into her. Yet another cry echoed inside her head, and Sarah

41

neither knew nor cared if it had sounded out loud or if it was just the disembodied echo of her absolute surrender.

'There!' she heard him gasp, and suddenly she was being filled as fully in the front as she was in the rear, and this living invader seemed to merge with the leather one, which felt as if it had sprung to life inside her. With all her strength she pulled against her bondage, eager to claim him and desperate to cling to him, but the thick leather was unyielding, pinning her wide like a trapped butterfly as his victorious spear began its pumping and thrusting dance of conquest.

Isobel de Lednay could barely suppress a grin of triumph as she followed the maidservant along the wide corridor and down the stairs into the cellar. Bressingham was a fool, and an arrogant one at that, and soon she would enjoy taking his money from him, of that she had no doubt.

She knew the Grayling estate quite well, having played here as a child with Ellen, and she had also seen two of these curious hunts before, so she knew well enough that although eventual capture was inevitable, the more resourceful quarry - whether dressed as birds, or deer or rabbits - managed to evade it for the better part of two hours, let alone one hour, and these were simple slave wenches probably terrified out of their wits and not thinking clearly, if they were capable of thinking at all.

Besides, the fact that they had endured hardships in their lives did not necessarily make them better fitted for running. Isobel had four brothers, two older and two younger, and she had learned to run and ride with them almost from the day she had first been able to walk. As an adult she was expected to follow more decorous pursuits, but she was confident she could still move fast enough to outwit a drunken dullard like Bressingham, in fact, she had just done exactly that.

She was also curious to know what it felt like to be set loose in one of those bizarre costumes, which were quite revealing and yet which showed little more than she would willingly display above her bodice at any social gathering. And did not the ladies of the French court bare their breasts as a matter of fashion?

Oh, yes, she told herself as she and her escort entered a room with a low ceiling at the end of the subterranean passageway, *this should be quite good fun, and there'll be a handsome payoff at the end of it to boot!*

James Calthorpe raised his head slowly above the top of the hedge, and peered across the deserted graveyard in the direction of the church.

Behind him, stooping low, Hannah Pennywise growled with frustration. 'What do you see?' she demanded.

James looked back down at the top of her head. 'Nothing,' he whispered, 'nothing at all. The church looks as if it's empty, and there is no one amongst the tombstones, at least no one I can see from here, but they could well be watching from the windows, and one man up in the bell tower could see the countryside for miles in all directions... ah, yes!' he hissed as he caught the first sign of movement. 'Yes, there *is* someone up there. I see only a shadow, but there is movement for sure. Yes, there he is again. A sentry for sure.' He ducked and slid down the few feet of embankment at the foot of the hedge. 'There's no way we can get close in daylight,' he affirmed. 'If what I heard is true and he now has more men with him, then I fear even with darkness as our ally any attempt to break in there would be doomed to failure.'

'Then I must pay the villain what he demands,' Hannah muttered.

'But what if he takes your gold and then kills you?' James said. 'He needn't even kill you outright. He could as easily buy testimony against you as Wickstanner must have done against Matilda.'

'Not if he thinks there's more where this came from.' Hannah held up the small leather pouch and jingled the contents.

'And is there?'

The old woman snorted. 'Oh, aye, aye, there's more, but whether it's enough for the likes of him, especially if he thinks he doesn't have the lot, who's to say?'

'Then you cannot allow yourself to fall into his clutches,' James declared. 'I'll go to him with an offer, half the gold now and the other half when he releases Matilda, and he can send an emissary to confirm we have the rest of the money.'

'A good idea,' Hannah agreed, 'but not you. Not you, nor me, for if he seizes either of us, then our numbers are cut in two at a stroke. No, we must find another to take the message and the gold, though not half, not to begin with. We'll send one fifth of what he first asked for, to show our good intent, and I think I know just who to despatch on such an errand. We'll send him during the funeral.'

'Yes, even Crawley would think twice before doing anything untoward before the entire village,' James agreed. 'Perhaps we should ask my father to take the message. His standing is such that—'

'No, not if Crawley already knows of your association with my Matilda,' Hannah cut him short. 'He might not dare to actually try to seize your father, but it would be better not to take the chance. No, I have a far better messenger in mind. Now, come lad,' she urged, turning stiffly, 'give me your arm until we're out of this lane. The ground here is so bad that I fear for my ankles and knees, and if I don't get some liniment onto them afore long, they'll surely seize up completely.'

'But this is preposterous!' Isobel stood defiantly, her cheeks blazing under the bird mask, as she sought in vain to cover her naked sex with wings designed not to come completely around in front of her body due to the tightness of the feathered jerkin between the shoulders, and its stiffness in the elbow joints. The maid who had dressed her stood waiting quietly, leaving things now to Grayling, whom she had summoned upon the red-haired noblewoman's insistence.

'But you agreed to the terms, my dear Isobel,' Grayling purred. 'You agreed you would be prepared exactly as the other girls have been.'

Isobel glared back at him, and then down at the strap with its attached tail and at the two dildos lying on the floor between them. 'But there was no way I could know about... about *those!*' she cried. 'That stupid girl there even tried to push them inside me, and oh... oh, Roderick, you know I had no idea, and you can make just one small allowance for an old friend. I can make it worth your while later after supper.' She tried to give him an encouraging smile, but the mask hid most of her features so it was largely a wasted effort.

'I count *two* allowances,' Grayling smirked, bending to scoop up the offending items. He appeared to examine them as if seeing them for the first time. 'Besides,' he added, 'whatever I say, Wormley will declare your wager lost, which will annoy those people with money riding on you, and Bressingham will certainly call foul.'

'But he need not know!' Isobel protested. 'He surely won't expect to examine me in such—'

'Probably not,' Grayling interrupted her, 'but he'll surely ask me to, and I'll have to give my word as a gentleman.'

'Pah, some gentleman *you* are, Roderick!'

'Perhaps it would be better if I did this for you?' Grayling suggested. 'I seem to remember a time not so very long ago...' He smiled.

Isobel held her defiant pose, but she knew when she was beaten, and she also knew Roderick was taking a certain amount of pleasure from her humiliation. He would certainly not let her off the hook, which would mean loss of face for her in front of all their friends, especially those who would lose their money if she did not carry the bet through. 'Very well,' she said finally, 'you do it, but first you can get on your knees and kiss me down there, as you've done willingly enough before. And then you can get some spittle on those beastly things, for I'll not have them in me dry, not unless you want to rip me in two, you awful beast, Roddy Grayling!'

On the inside of the fence, the woods seemed as quiet and deserted as on the outside. Paddy had sawn through the selected paling with deliberate care, although to Toby, crouched watching and listening a good fifty yards further along the boundary, each saw cut had seemed abnormally loud, and he had been sure that at any moment the Grayling keepers must come bursting through the trees.

'You've not been this far in lately, I suppose?' Paddy whispered as Toby padded up alongside him. 'It might be just as well if you went back now then.'

Toby shook his head firmly. 'No,' he said, 'I'm staying with you. I'm the only one who knows what Miss Harriet looks like, don't forget, and anyway, who says I ain't been in here lately.'

'You mean you have?'

Toby nodded, smirking. 'That fence was intended to keep out the likes of you and Mister Kelly here. Someone my size can find several places where the rails are far enough apart not to need no sawing. Don't you worry, sergeant sir, I knows my way around these woods well enough, at least to within a distance of the house, and I also knows where the keepers patrol usually.' He pointed off to the right. 'There's a pathway runs from one end to the other just down there a-ways. It's wide, wide enough that Lady Ellen sometimes takes a trap ride along it, or at least she used to. The keepers use it to ride their horses; saves them doing too much on foot, see.'

'Makes sense.' Paddy nodded. 'So, which way is the house from here, left or right?'

'Just to the left,' Toby said, 'but it's a good couple of miles and the undergrowth is a bit too thick if we try to go in a straight line. Best way is to find that main path and then head off into the trees a bit and follow it for about a mile that way.' He waved an arm to indicate a direction further to the left. 'Round about there another path goes off towards the house. It's a bit winding, but we can follow a straighter line through the trees as they ain't anywhere near as thick there.'

'What about the keepers?'

Toby shook his head. 'Can't be sure,' he replied. 'Usually they stay out near the fence, waiting to catch anyone trying to get in, but there ain't so many of them this time of day as most poachers work at night.'

'Aye, we know that, Toby lad,' Sean Kelly grinned at him, 'but these sods ain't just watching for poachers, methinks, so we'd best watch our steps carefully.' He looked down, and gave his musket an affectionate pat. 'We'll just have to show these English bastards how these things are really done, won't we, me darling?'

What had at first seemed to her like an adventure and an easy way of taking money off that idiot, Guy Bressingham, was now taking on the proportions of a nightmarish ordeal, as far as Isobel de Lednay was concerned. She cursed herself for her foolishness - for not being more sure of her facts, and for not fully understanding what the bird-girls were expected to endure. The twin dildos lodged inside her now seemed to mock her carelessness as she followed the maidservant back out into daylight, where she was received with a round of applause that was as much ribald as it was appreciative.

Isobel would have readily delivered a torrent of castigating abuse at her supposed friends, but the gag - yet another refinement she had failed to consider - prevented her from uttering anything beyond an incomprehensible grunt, and she was determined not to give Bressingham, or any of the others, the satisfaction of realising the full extent of her helplessness. Her eyes narrowed behind the mask and she vowed to exact a suitably vindictive revenge on her former lover, Grayling, as soon as the opportunity presented itself.

Grayling himself, having performed the duty of inserting the dildos, had left the maid to gag Isobel and was thus already back on the lawn when she made her entrance. He nodded at her, and then at one of the grooms, who

45

immediately took charge of her and guided her to the other bird-girls. She bit deeply into the gag and steeled herself to walk as naturally as the weighted boots and the two invaders permitted, fighting back the small spasms that every step triggered inside her.

Damn Roddy, she thought, and damn herself for being so stupid. Even the boots had come as a shock when she tried to walk in them for the first time. Outwardly, they gave no indication of the way in which they were weighted, and for the first time she began to doubt herself, for the footwear presented a handicap she had not bargained on. Yet if these stupid peasant girls could stay free for over two hours, and occasionally even longer than that, then she could certainly evade capture for the required hour. She would then be released to claim her prize, and to savour Bressingham's defeat for the rest of the day and well into the evening.

'You know what you have to do, Billy Dodds?' Hannah Pennywise leaned close to the young lad's face and peered into his eyes.

He stared back at her, his unblinking eyes plainly reflecting his awe of her. 'Yes, mistress, don't worry none, I can do this as well as Toby would have, maybe even better.' The news that Toby Blaine had disappeared somewhere - and nobody was saying where the boy had gone, only that he was not expected back for several hours - had come as a blow to Hannah. Toby was a bright lad, sometimes too quick with his lip, but dependable and honest enough, if you didn't count poaching the odd rabbit or two, which nobody in their right mind would. Billy Dodds, usually all but inseparable from Toby, was the obvious substitute, the only real alternative, Hannah knew, and she hoped the lad was even half as bright as his friend. 'You do it just after they lower the coffin, you understand?' she repeated.

Billy nodded. 'Yeah, I hand the bag over and give him the note and tell him I'll be outside the inn an hour later. That's it, isn't it?'

'Yes, that's exactly it,' James said reassuringly. 'Everything else is in the note, so all you have to do is deliver it and then get away and come back here to the cottage. I'll be watching, and so will most of the village, so you won't be in any danger.'

'I just don't much like the look of the fellow,' Billy muttered. 'Looks like he's already dead, if'n you ask me.'

'And acts like he should be,' Hannah agreed, 'so you just make sure you get your tail out of there as soon as you've delivered bag, note and message.'

'And I get a half-crown for this?' Billy asked suspiciously.

Hannah and James nodded in unison as she delved into the folds of her skirt and pulled out a coin. 'And this is a shilling of it,' she said, pressing it into Billy's grubby palm. 'Mind you,' she added fiercely, 'you let us down and I'll not only have it back off you, I'll have the skin off your back and maybe something else to boot. You understand me?' One look at the expression on Billy's face was enough to answer her question.

46

Crawley's new recruits had finally seemed to lose interest in her, if only temporarily, but in truth Harriet realised she had passed beyond caring any more. Her body ached in every joint and muscle, but even those pains had subsided to a dull numbness that mimicked that of her brain, and although she felt exhausted in every way, she knew also that sleep would not come now, nor would she dare surrender to it even if it did.

Her mouth felt dry and sour, her tongue stiff and sore from the constant assault of the metal prong, and she wondered if any of them would bother to think about giving her water. Probably not if Crawley intended to hang her. Dully, she looked up, craning her neck towards the narrow slit of glass... it was still daylight outside, she saw, but the combination of dirt and weeds growing up against the side of the building made it impossible to even guess at how far the day had advanced, or even whether it was sunny.

Sunset. One of the men - or had it been Crawley himself? - had said they would be hanging her at sunset, but somehow the prospect had failed to penetrate her general horror. Now she began to consider this, and as she did so, tears formed in her eyes, tears that were not for herself but for Oliver, her father. If they killed her, who would care for him? Who would tend the farm? Thomas Handiwell was a good and kind man, but she doubted his interest would continue beyond her death, for his only duty to her father would have come through her if she had agreed to his proposal of marriage.

Thomas. Jane. Jane Handiwell. Was it really possible that Jane was...? But of course it was, for had not the girl told Harriet so herself? Yet she still found it hard to believe it even though she knew Jane hated her personally and saw her as a threat to her inheritance of the inn. But hate, suspicion, jealousy, all those were understandable even if they were not Christian, whereas robbery and kidnapping, and on such a scale... Jane Handiwell, Ellen Grayling, Mary Watling and especially Kate Dawson, who outwardly appeared to be such a mousy and characterless individual... it seemed to Harriet that the entire world must have gone mad.

Crawley was certainly mad, she knew, though mad in a cold and zealous way carrying with it a power and persuasiveness that could spread wider and wider if no one was prepared to take a stand against it. The Jacob Crawley's of the world were more dangerous than the worst highwayman, murderer or thief, for they truly believed the wickedness they purveyed was not wickedness at all but an instrument of divine justice.

Or did they?

Matilda's grandmother had been mentioned more than once, Harriet now realised, and there had been mention also of a payment. She shook her head, and urged her fatigued mind to concentrate. Payment... some kind of ransom? Her eyes narrowed. Yes, there had long been talk in and around the village that Hannah Pennywise had a hidden hoard of gold left her by her father. Nathan and the old woman had never shown even the slightest sign of profligacy, so his bequest must surely still be intact, assuming it existed at all.

Jacob Crawley might not be an instrument of God, even if only a self-appointed instrument, quite so much as an ordinarily greedy monster seeking an earthly reward rather than eternal salvation. Harriet grunted. Ordinary human failings she could understand, and the realisation that Crawley was really no more than a common thief made him appear suddenly less awesome, although not, she told herself grimly, any less dangerous. He still held her life in his hands, and time must surely be running out.

And then another memory came back to her, although she could not at first be sure it was a real memory and not a dream. She had a stark vision of herself being thrown into this room, the leather hood pulled over her face and laced tight, the terrible scold's bridle locked over it, and then there was a swirling cloud of pain and shadow, a cloud through which a light had come, and a face, and a voice... 'You'll go on your way with something to remember me by,' the voice had grated, and then an awful ordeal followed accompanied by the shock that such a thing could be happening to her. Eventually, her mind had rebelled, refusing to acknowledge the reality of her plight, and she fainted away.

Something to remember me by.

Oh, she would remember that, and she would remember him all right. How could any woman ever hope to banish such memories?

Something to remember me by.

How could she ever forget?

Something to remember...

And yet there *was* something she had forgotten, or rather something that had made no sense to her stunned mind at the time. Now, however, it began to come back to Harriet, and she recalled stories her father had told her of his time in the eastern counties, especially the time he had been garrisoned at... Colchester? Yes, Colchester. He said there had been trials and executions there that at first were sanctioned by the Church, spreading terror through the countryside and inciting a wave of public piety that was much more about saving one's body than one's eternal soul. And then even the Church and its bishops had come to their senses, for their ecclesiastical lordships were not so far removed from reality as not to realise when something had gone too far. Oliver Merridew himself had led a detachment out to a village near the coast to stop the intended execution of three supposed witches, two old women and a young girl barely of childbearing age. There had nearly been a riot in which three villagers, and a member of Oliver's troops, was killed. It had been the last of the executions, the last of the madness, the last of the trials, at least in that part of the country, and the man responsible had vanished from the area overnight almost as if he had never existed. There had been stories of him, or at least of someone bearing the same name, reappearing further north about a year later. Harriet always read the newssheets, even if they were usually two weeks old before they reached Leddingham, and then nothing more was heard of him.

The world at large had heaved a sigh of relief, at least that part of the world where the maniac had spread his reign of terror. Some said he fled to France and that there was a price on his head. Others said he himself had been executed, though the stories differed as to whether he died in Scotland or in France or even in Yorkshire. Still others believed he had taken ship for the New World, or that he became a missionary to the Dark Continent. But whatever the truth, all agreed on one thing - if his name was never heard again in England it would be the greatest blessing God could give his children.

Something to remember me by... Something to remember, something that no one could ever hope to forget... *or my name isn't Matthew Hopkins.*

Harriet felt a chill run down her spine and numb her legs. *Matthew Hopkins!* That was the name of the madman who had killed scores of innocents in the name of God, the name that the sane and civilised world had thought never to hear again, and now...

Surely not, she thought desperately. Yet had she not heard it from his own lips? She was certain now it had been no dream. Jacob Crawley and Matthew Hopkins, the hated and feared persecutor of innocents, the man who had put a rope around the necks of old women and children alike... Jacob Crawley and Matthew Hopkins were one and the same person, and now the rope was about to go round Harriet's own neck!

Ellen Grayling lay back against the pile of pillows at the head of her bed and grinned at Jane Handiwell. 'Janey, my dear,' she drawled, 'you look so impressive in that darling outfit, but what say you *do* catch one of the birdies? You aren't exactly equipped for the ritual stuffing.'

Jane, who was dressed in a black leather jerkin, breeches and boots, and who was now in the process of pulling a matching hood over her head, grinned back at her aristocratic young friend. 'Ellie dear,' she replied smoothly, 'there is more than one way to skin a cat, and certainly more than one way to stuff a bird, as I thought you should know well enough by now.'

'Of course, my darling,' Ellen replied, 'but not down in the main hall, and not in front of all those beastly friends of Roddy's. It might suit for one of those great sweaty men to stick his cock into a slave in public, but we're supposed to be ladies.'

'The rules don't say the bird has to be stuffed in public.' Jane smiled and peered out from two narrow slits angled to give the mask an almost oriental appearance. Only her mouth and chin remained uncovered. 'Besides,' she added, 'I can let Oona do the public show. I always find it so amusing when those silly birds realise her little secret.'

Ellen gave a visible shudder. 'That creature makes my skin crawl. She's not human, I'm sure of it, and one of these days she'll end up killing someone. I do wish Roddy wouldn't put those claw things on her hands; she's dangerous enough without them. Have you seen those two fangs up close?'

'I think she's a handsome specimen,' Jane retorted. 'She has the most beautiful body, so strong and athletic, and her features beneath all the paint and the masks... well, there's something very individual about her.'

'Thank the Lord for that!' Ellen exclaimed. 'To think there could ever be another like her!'

'Perhaps, if Roddy would permit us, we should try to tame her a little?' Jane suggested.

For a moment Ellen could not be sure her friend was serious, and when she realised she was, her expression became even more horrified. 'You can't mean that? Why, Jane Handiwell, is there no shame in you? You look at that demented half-human creature and all you see is an adventure in your bed. Shame on you!'

'Why, Ellie, I do believe you might be jealous.' Jane's thin lips curled back in a spiteful grin. 'The thought of my little pussy taking any cock is too much for you to bear, isn't it? Well, I doubt it would ever happen anyway. Even I would be wary of Oona when her shaft appears, for the lust in her eyes signals danger, to be sure. No, Oona can sate herself on the slaves. But today I shall be her handler, so I shall need to scent myself heavily. You know what she's like if the smell of female becomes too strong in her nostrils. Although she knows just which females are game, I still wouldn't trust her if she became too frustrated.'

'Then make sure you carry a stout cane and a good thick whip,' Ellen urged. 'Beat her at the first sign of trouble, and don't be afraid to call for help.'

'Then why don't you come out with me?' Jane suggested. 'We can show those men a thing or two between us, I'm sure.'

'I'm sure we could,' Ellen agreed, 'but you know what Roddy is like about things like that. In public, I must remain the dainty and silly little lady just in case anyone was to think anything else and perhaps suspect something. He even protests if I ride out in breeches on a proper saddle during the daytime, so I have to be very careful to keep out of his sight if I do other than he wishes.'

'Wait until he settles down with his two little black bitches. I cannot for the life of me understand how he can let those two barbarians into his sight, let alone let them suckle on his cock as he does.'

'Oh, I don't know,' Ellen sighed, 'they are perfectly tame and really quite sweet. Besides, those big lips do look so soft...'

'Ellen Grayling, you are worse even than I. Next thing you'll be telling me is that you've taken one of them into your own bed and...' Her voice trailed off seeing the expression on Ellen's face, and turning on her heel, she strode towards the door. 'I'm not going to continue with this conversation,' she said, 'for I suspect I might not like the answers you give, and there are some things best left unasked, I think.'

Harriet had been awakened from an uneasy sleep, this time by Crawley himself. The witchfinder kicked her thigh with the toe of his boot and instructed her to rise.

Awkwardly, feeling the cold in every one of her stiff joints, Harriet obeyed.

Crawley stood facing her and looking her up and down, a malicious grin on his hawkish features. 'Doesn't look like there's much of the devil in you now, does there, wench? Mind, it wouldn't do to let the poor fools out there know that. There's not a body among them as doesn't reckon it's you made Wickstanner put the rope round his neck and jump the way he did.'

Harriet's eyes grew round at this revelation, for it was the first time anyone had mentioned Wickstanner's death to her.

'Aye, well, whether you did or didn't, I reckon the blame can be laid before you fair enough anyway. The man was a weak fool, and somehow you managed to get inside his stupid head to mess with his thoughts, and that's why he did himself in, no mistake about it. So it'll be fair and square, an eye for an eye, when we hang you tonight.'

Harriet whimpered, but there was no way in which she could otherwise communicate with her tormentor.

'Ha, well, you might be scared, but it'll be painless enough, just a quick drop. Of course, if the old witch you call your grandmother still refuses to pay by the time dusk comes, then maybe we'll get the drop wrong, and maybe there'll be a little jig for her to watch.' He reached out and grasped Harriet's nipples cruelly between his thumb and forefingers. 'I've sent a man to find her with that message, but it seems she's disappeared into thin air for he reports there's no sign of life at her cottage. Not that it'll help her much, for she'll be the next one to swing, and the miller's lad too. Jed Mardley's body was discovered in a hut in the woods and there's witnesses that both the crone and the lad were out that way, so once we've dealt with you, we'll have to deal with them too.'

Harriet blinked as she struggled to take in everything Crawley was saying. That he still thought she was Matilda was obvious, for the mask and the spike branch prevented either recognition or appeal. That he had originally taken Matilda in collusion with Wickstanner was also not surprising, and neither was the apparent admission that greed for gold had more to do with his actions than a genuine belief Matilda had offended the Church, despite his occasional references to the devil. With Wickstanner dead, that now left Crawley in complete control of both church and village, at least from a spiritual point of view, and the ease with which he had recruited additional support was testimony to the greed and ignorance of a certain element of humanity. But that one of his original cohorts had died and he was preparing to lay a case against Hannah Pennywise and James Calthorpe as a result meant that if Hannah did in fact come forward in an attempt to buy Matilda's life, she would be walking straight into a trap.

Did Hannah still labour under the misapprehension that Crawley was holding her granddaughter and preparing to execute her? If the old woman had been in any way connected with swapping herself for Matilda (perhaps she had paid Jane and her friends to do the deed in the first place) might that not explain the old woman's disappearance? She and Matilda would surely be many miles away by now and unlikely to return until long after they were sure Crawley had left the area. In that case, there would be no attempt to pay a ransom, and even though it was obvious Crawley did not intend to release his prisoner anyway, if the money he demanded did not arrive, he would be very angry.

Harriet shuddered.

Isobel de Lednay was not only beginning to regret her impulsive wager (she had begun to regret it even before the maid finished fitting her bird tunic and mask) she was beginning to regret not withdrawing from it before it had become too late to do so.

Now, with a gag strapped into her mouth beneath the beak (she had protested and tried to resist this, but to no avail) further argument was impossible, and she knew there was nothing for it but to run with the other bird girls when the order was given.

The guests had watched her humiliation with a curious mixture of anticipation and stunned silence. Even the usually brash and obnoxious Bressingham seemed at a loss for words and made no comment when Grayling insisted she wear these awful nipple clamps with their attached bells. He pointed out that as the other girls had nipple rings it would give her an unfair advantage if she also were not obliged to wear them. 'At least I'm not insisting your teats be pierced, my sweet,' he had murmured as he tightened the round clamps, 'but we can't have totally silent birds in the woods, otherwise how will the hunters know where to start looking?' He then completed her ensemble by tying a length of ribbon between the rings, which would distinguish her from the other birds so only Bressingham would be permitted to hunt her.

'However,' he announced to the gathering, 'if any other hunters see this pretty bird, they are at liberty to let Bressingham know where she is lurking.'

A large hourglass filled with sand had been brought out from the house and set up on a small table in the centre of the lawn. Isobel saw the glass had been marked in several places, both at the top and at the bottom, and that the sand currently in the lower section would apparently take four hours to run through. She, however, only had to remain at liberty until the first hour's passing was marked.

'When the first hour is up,' Grayling announced, 'I shall instruct the bell in the tower to be rung ten times. Its sound can be heard everywhere in the grounds and a good deal further, so there will be no mistaking when, or if, the wager has been completed.' He turned to where the actual hunters had gathered. The deadly-looking Oona squatted before a black-garbed figure who held her leash, and Isobel realised it was a female, although she was tall for a woman and her breasts were either small or bound flat against her chest beneath the leather jerkin. 'And now it is time. The birds are allowed a head start of four minutes. I shall count to two-hundred-and-fifty at a steady pace to make sure.'

The bird-girls shuffled uneasily, eyeing each other as if wondering whether or not they should already be running and glancing at Oona, whose hands had been encased in strange glove-like pouches from which a steel claw projected at the end of each finger.

Isobel turned her head to peer out at Grayling from her bird head, and he seemed to be looking directly at her.

He raised a hand, and glanced back at the spectators, playing the drama to its full. 'If we're ready then,' he said, and dropping his hand with a flourish cried, 'Run, you little feathered whores!'

Sarah nearly collapsed when Ross finally released and lifted her down from her terrible perch. Her knees buckled, the strength drained from every muscle by the prolonged and wracking orgasms her captor had inflicted upon her. Now, as he indicated for her to kneel before him, she was only too willing to obey. His manhood rose up straight and stiff despite the rigours to which it had subjected her as he leaned forward and unbuckled her gag strap, pulling the sodden and chewed wedge of leather out from between her teeth. She knew without being told what was now expected of her.

Closing her eyes, she bobbed her head forward until she felt the head of his weapon bump against her lips. Slowly, she allowed her lips to slide over his taut, hot flesh until she had taken his head entirely into her mouth and it was pressing firmly against her tongue. The taste of it was at once salty and sweet, and Sarah realised she must in fact be sucking on her own juices. Ross grasped her head, forcing himself further into her reluctant mouth, and she all but gagged as his shaft pushed towards the back of her throat.

'Make some effort now, my little bitch slave.'

Reluctantly, she drew back until only the tip of his erection was between her lips, and then she plunged forward again, sucking firmly as she did so.

'That's more like it... just keep that up, there's a good girl.'

Sarah screwed her eyes tightly closed and began to work at the task with a slow rhythm that was rewarded by matching strokes of her hair by his fingers.

'That's very good,' he said, and it seemed his voice had risen somewhat.

She wondered if he was going to show the same restraint and control he had displayed during his prolonged fucking, or if he was now going to pay her the ultimate insult, having refused to come inside her body only to spend in her hapless mouth. Her answer was not long in coming.

'Faster now,' he urged, thrusting forward to meet her movements and almost choking her in the process. 'That's it... damn you, you little bitch, but you have a soft mouth!'

Sarah whimpered around her flesh-and-blood gag, but now she did not dare stop, and having come this far she began fiercely telling herself it no longer mattered, that anything was better than the punishments she had both received and witnessed. The air in this gloomy and bizarre little chamber seemed more oppressive than ever, and the only thought she now had was to please this beast and hopefully get out of this place as soon as possible.

'That's it,' Ross gasped, and an instant later she felt her throat being sprayed with his hot, salty seed. She tried to pull back, but his hands grasped the back of her neck and held her to him, and she knew he would not release her until she performed the ultimate act. With a choking sob, Sarah swallowed.

Matilda stumbled several times during the first few yards of her run, but she quickly realised that haste meant less speed and so she reduced her run to a short striding canter and began to take greater stock of her surroundings.

Already the house and lawn were well hidden from view. The trees were tall and grew close together, and the undergrowth ranged from low-lying brambles to large, sprawling bushes taller than she was. The place truly was a wilderness, and but for pathways cut fairly clearly by human hands, she could have been in the depths of the most remote countryside weeks away from civilisation.

The bells hanging from her nipple rings kept up a constant jingling as she ran, and there was no way she could bring her arms around far enough to suppress the sound. She tried calculating how much time had passed since she began running. She guessed maybe half of the four minutes must have elapsed, yet the time could just as easily be up and the bells would give her away if she was still moving once the hunters began approaching.

She staggered to a halt, panting heavily and looking wildly around. Before her the trail forked left and right, but unless she wanted to risk remaining on the open pathways and offering no option to her pursuers other than a simple this way or that, she would have to risk making her way through the forest itself. Perhaps, she thought, there would be other turns after the fork, but there was little time now in which to find out. Assuming the hunters could run twice as fast as she could, she had less than five minutes before they would be able to hear her, and once they got a bearing on her position, she was unlikely to escape their clutches for long. Turning, she began to lope along the pathway again.

All the bird-girls had been directed to enter the woods at different points, so there was little chance of a hunter who chose her route stumbling across another victim to distract him. She had to find cover, but there seemed no way to make progress through such dense foliage. Praying the trees would thin out a little before long, she hesitated only for a moment when she came to the fork in the path before swinging off to the right. She almost cried out with relief when only a few paces along her chosen path the greenery on her right suddenly thinned out. A long clearing stretched at right angles to the path, and unless she was imagining things, several other narrower trails appeared to lead away from it at irregular intervals.

Breathing hard, Matilda ran into the middle of the clearing, cursing the jingling bells and the constant pulling and jerking on her tender nipples. She had tried all along to ignore the hard leather phalluses, but as she ran they seemed to come alive inside her. Air whistled through the holes in her mask as she paused to try to get some air back into her aching lungs, and she used this brief interlude to try and think. She counted seven different paths leading away from the clearing, none of them very wide, and there was no guarantee they might not all peter out after only a few yards. However, if she kept thinking like this then she might as well give up now, and she had been warned what became of girls who allowed themselves to be caught too easily.

Whether the paths led anywhere, more important was whether her pursuers knew if they did or not, or if their knowledge of the grounds was as sparse as her own. If the latter was the case, then the seven routes offered Matilda odds of seven to one, odds that, with any degree of luck, should give her a reasonable chance of remaining at large for more than an hour, perhaps even two. If she did choose a dead end, then she would go to ground and try to lay quiet in the hope that anyone who happened to follow the same path might not feel inclined to search too thoroughly.

The last exit seemed the obvious choice since it would take her the furthest away from the hunting area... too obvious, she decided, for if she was followed this far, the hunter might realise her initial choice at the fork had been made with exactly this thought in mind. Two pathways to her right seemed to lead back in the approximate direction of the house, so she discounted those as well, although not before she allowed herself another couple of seconds to consider whether this fact alone might put off a would-be captor. In the end, she decided it would be too confining if she did go back that way, and after only an instant's hesitation she plunged down the central path to her left. She almost caught her foot against a trailing tree root, and flapping wildly to keep her balance silently cursed the bells, the tree, and above all the wickedness that had brought her to this pass.

All the while as she ran, the image in her mind of the awful dog-woman began to grow, the fang-like teeth appearing to elongate in her mental picture, the baleful, predatory eyes seeming to shine with a sinister light...

Isobel was faring no better than Matilda even though she began her run where the trees had seemed a little thinner and there was less growth underneath. However, after the first minute or so the forest began to close in on her, so when she came to the first turn she decided to take it in the hope that it would bring her around away from the denser areas.

For about another two minutes it seemed her tactic had been a success, but although the trees remained well spaced, the bushes and brambles began to close in on her now and she was forced to slow to little more than a walk. She also had to jump over several tangled outcrops, an action that set her breasts bouncing uncomfortably and the attached nipple bells ringing loudly.

She came to a halt, her winged arms hanging limply at her sides, air wheezing in and out of the narrow nostril openings in her mask, and was astonished to feel a surge of heat shoot upwards from her groin. She staggered sideways, all but losing her balance, and gasped around her gag as she realised the sensation was a fierce orgasm brought on by the dual attentions of the dildos Roderick Grayling had inserted into her with such enthusiasm. Tottering away from what path there was, she fell against the nearest tree, leaning on it for support as the waves of painful pleasure began to subside.

Damn Grayling and his leather cocks, she thought, and damn her own body for surrendering so easily to their presence. At this rate she would have no hope of outrunning Bressingham, and aside from the interruptions her strength would also soon become completely sapped. With a groan that was as much determination as discomfort, she straightened up and looked around, but the second she tried to walk again the two shafts lodged inside her immediately threatened to cause another collapse.

Isobel shook her head and tried desperately to concentrate on which way she should go now, telling herself to ignore everything from the waist down. She should be able to control her own body, especially when the things inside her were not in any way real. Finally, after what felt like several minutes but which in fact was only twenty seconds or so, she tried to walk again, biting deeply into the leather gag as she began moving towards what appeared to be a thinner area of bushes.

The heat was still there, but now thoughts of Bressingham - who must even now be starting after her - began to override all other considerations. When the tangle beneath her boots eventually did give way to grass and hard mud, she found she could manage a brisk trot.

Jane Handiwell had been fascinated by the dog-woman, Oona, since the very first time she laid eyes on her, although she knew that to describe the wild creature as feminine was not exactly accurate. Oona's firm breasts, flaring hips and prominent sex made her gender obvious, but Jane had seen her when she was aroused. The first time the sinister brown shaft began to emerge from the little African's vagina, she had assumed it to be just a malformed and overdeveloped clitoris. However, when the monstrous thing continued to grow and stiffen until it stood out, and up, a good eight or nine inches, Jane realised that Oona was equipped with as superb a cock as any man, and that she was that great a rarity - a genuine hermaphrodite. Oona not only possessed the equipment she also possessed a great appetite. The faintest scent of a female in a state of arousal was enough to bring a growl from her throat that gradually rose in pitch until it became a predatory howl that sent shivers down the spines of all who heard it.

For the moment, however, Oona loped along in her usual curious fashion, not quite running on all fours but bent forward at the hip so her clawed fingers all but scraped the ground before her. The long leather leash from her collar led back to where Jane had wound it about her wrist, and as Ellen suggested, she carried a whip-cane in her other hand with a short but heavy whip coiled at her hip. Oona was human enough and intelligent enough to know the difference between hunter and hunted, but Jane was not taking any chances.

The pair had initially chosen one of the more central paths, accompanied by a male hunter, but when the path divided the fellow decided to take the left turn and Jane had not bothered to suggest to him that Oona's nose was probably a far better guide than his instincts.

'Hold there, Oona!' she cried now as the dog-girl suddenly lunged forward. She pulled firmly back on the leash, jerking the creature's head up, and when the baleful eyes turned towards her she lifted the cane in an unmistakable gesture. 'Steady, I say!' she snapped. 'No need to rush, you stupid animal. You may find it easy enough to run over this ground, but I most certainly do not. Now, let's see where we are.'

Oona squatted obediently, waiting for the command to move off again as Jane turned slowly in a half circle, trying to fix a map in her mind. She knew these woods as well as anyone and knew also that it was possible to run around in circles almost blindly and miss several short cuts. From where they were - in an area that was not quite a clearing, but certainly not anywhere near as overgrown as most of the surrounding area - Jane knew there were only two real routes their quarry could take. Oona seemed to want to go right, but that way became a path barely two feet wide and with no obvious ways off it for perhaps a mile. At the same time, it wound around in a great loop and came back around to where the path on the left could take them by a far more direct route.

'We'll let the silly bitch run her legs out,' Jane said dryly. She gathered some of the leash and tugged Oona around, pointing with the cane the way she wanted to go. To her surprise, the dog-girl seemed not only to understand but also to agree, panting and growling softly in the back of her throat. 'Not quite as dumb as they treat you, I see.' Jane chuckled. 'Well, maybe you're even a lot cleverer than that. You'd know these ways by now, probably almost as well as I, so let's move on and head our girl off around about where the stream rises from the foot of the hill. And don't worry, my little pagan beauty, you shall have first reward with her when we catch her. After being skewered on that fine cock of yours, she'll be nice and docile for me.' And probably grateful enough to have been delivered from Oona's clutches to do just about anything she demanded of her, Jane reflected, unable to suppress a grin of anticipation.

Paddy Riley's eyes almost popped out of his head when the curious bird woman suddenly burst out of the bushes before them, explaining the curious jingling sounds he knew should have been enough to warn them to proceed with more caution. He was so taken aback that for a moment his military training completely deserted him and he stood frozen in astonishment. Behind him, both Sean Kelly and Toby Blaine were similarly brought up short.

Before any of them could react, the woman turned and dove back into the undergrowth, the ringing of her bouncing bells echoing in the air behind her, and then gradually fading into the twittering of birds in the branches high above them.

'Did you see that?' Kelly gasped, moving up to Paddy's shoulder. His eyes were as round as saucers and there was a curious half smile on his face.

Paddy snorted. 'Of course I saw it, you damned fool. Do you think I'm as blind as you are deaf? Didn't you hear the bell things on her tits? I'm a damned fool, and so are you, Sean Kelly. That could have been anything we just walked into!'

'Well, it was certainly something!' Kelly exclaimed. 'D'you think she's off to tell we're here?'

Riley narrowed his eyes and shook his head. 'I doubt that,' he said soberly. 'Didn't look as if she was in any fit state to tell about anything, and she was running away from something herself.'

'Then who do you think she was?' Kelly persisted.

Riley shook his head in a gesture of disbelief. 'And how the hell would I be knowing that?' he demanded. 'Did you not see the wench was wearing that mask thing, and if you think I'm after identifying women from the shape of their tits and other bodily parts, well then Sean Kelly, I think maybe you've gone a little soft in the head.'

'It's a sort of hunting game they play.' Toby Blaine moved up on Paddy's other side. 'We've seen them before, back last summer. There were lots of them all dressed up like she was as birds, and the hunters are all in black with hoods and masks so you couldn't see their faces. They carry pistols and whips, but I don't know whether they really shoot them, 'cos we didn't wait around to see. Billy got scared when we nearly ran into one of the hunters and we hightailed it back to the fence, though I wanted to wait and see what happened.'

'I'll just bet you did.' Paddy grinned. He had taken an instant liking to the lad, and he could easily imagine what had gone through the youngster's head the first time he had seen one of these bizarre creatures. Riley himself had seen plenty of things, but the few seconds of confrontation with the bird- girl had more than stirred up his manhood. 'The thing is,' he went on, 'this could make our job just a little bit harder than we might have expected. If they have Mistress Harriet running around in one of those bird things, then how is Toby here to know her? I doubt he'd be any better at recognising a pair of... mother of heaven, what am I saying?'

'So what do we do?' Sean Kelly asked. 'We'd better be careful if there's fellows out chasing with guns. They might end up shooting at us by mistake.'

'If they shoot at us,' Paddy said grimly, 'it won't be a matter of any mistake, to be sure. There's no way anyone with eyes is going to confuse the likes of you and me with the likes of *that!*' He nodded his head in the direction in which the girl had plunged back into the woods. 'No, we'd not be mistaken for one like that,' he continued, 'but I do have an idea what we might be mistaken for.'

With the two Irish troopers and Toby the only real chance of making any progress as far as the Grayling estate was concerned, and with the small likelihood of any news from Portsmouth arriving before sundown, Thomas Handiwell at last turned his attention to the other events in the village. It was a way of killing time and trying, albeit vainly, to take his mind from what might have happened, or be happening, to Harriet. Had he known, his course of action would have doubtless been very different and much more direct, but like the rest of the village, he believed the unfortunate girl awaiting execution in the church was Matilda Pennywise.

Thomas had only seen Matilda on a handful of occasions and had only ever exchanged a brief nod with her in passing. Since arriving in Leddingham from London, she had never set foot in the *Drum* and was seldom, if ever, out late. However, he had known her grandmother for many years, and Hannah's father, Nathan, had known his own father since before Thomas's was born. And now, as he listened to Ned's summary of events, he began to feel guilty that he had not done anything earlier. Being neither religious nor superstitious, Thomas did not believe in witches, and as he told Ned, even if he did, Hannah Pennywise certainly wasn't one. And as for her granddaughter, the fool vicar had been sniffing round her skirts for months, and if a vicar couldn't see a witch at ten paces, then who in hell's name could?

Leaving Hart at the inn - the young officer point-blank refused to become embroiled in affairs of the church, no matter how preposterous they were - and charging him to come after him the moment there was any news, Thomas set off into the village and made straight for the church. At the main door he found his way barred by Alfred Diggins and Peter Farren. Both men carried muskets and sported pistols tucked into their belts.

'Tell this Master Crawley I wish to speak with him.' Thomas spoke quietly but firmly, not in the least awed by the weaponry. He knew both these men from the inn and doubted they were as familiar with guns, let alone real fighting, as they were trying to appear, and he could smell drink on the breath of both of them.

'The gentleman has given instructions that he's not to be disturbed and no one is to enter here meantime, Master Handiwell,' Alfred Diggins drawled.

Thomas sniffed. 'Alfred,' he said carefully, fixing the fellow with an unblinking stare, 'this witchfinder fellow will like as not be gone tomorrow, or the day after, but I doubt you will, and I know the *Black Drum* will be where it stands for many years to come. Now, if you harbour even the most slender hope of ever drinking in my inn again, you will kindly take your shiftless frame and tell this *gentleman* that I have business with him.'

Diggins, although lazy by nature and not very sharp, was nevertheless quite capable of understanding a threat. The next nearest source of alcohol was a good twelve miles down the road towards the coast, and he was not about to get himself banned from his usual watering hole. It was with ill grace that he turned, swung open one half of the church door, and disappeared inside. But disappear he did, leaving Thomas alone with Peter Farren.

'I must say, Peter,' Thomas remarked sourly, "tis a surprise to find you in a church and no mistaking.'

Farren shifted his weight and blinked, but the gold already in his pocket, and the promise of more to come, had given him more resolve than he usually had to draw upon. 'I might say the same of you, Master Handiwell,' he replied. 'You're not best known around here for a regular attendance in the Lord's house.'

'I'll not deny the truth in that,' Thomas retorted, 'but at least I earn my own corn and don't turn my coat to something just because some fellow in a cassock jingles a few coins.'

'Master Crawley don't wear no cassock, innkeeper, and he ain't no priest, neither. He's appointed special by the lord bishops up in London. I knows that 'cos he showed us his warrant.'

'And read it out for you, I suppose?' Handiwell sneered. He knew full well that Peter Farren, in common with most of the villagers, could neither read nor write and would easily enough be impressed with any scroll that contained well drawn letters and a seal.

Further conversation was rendered unnecessary, however, for the door opened again and Crawley himself emerged. His eyes looked red, and there were huge dark bags beneath them, but he carried himself erect and there was a presence about him that Thomas could see would both impress and intimidate the simple village folk. He stepped out alone, but behind him stood the shadowy figure of Diggins, and that of a second man.

'What brings a seller of the devil's brew to the house of God?' Crawley demanded. 'They tell me your shadow never usually touches this portal, Master Handiwell.'

'Indeed it seldom does, Master Crawley,' Thomas replied easily, 'but then this house has never before contained such foolishness. The girl, Matilda Pennywise... rumour has it you intend to hang her this evening?'

''Tis no rumour, Master Handiwell. The whore wench is a heretic and has been seen practising the dark arts. She is possessed of wickedness, of a vile spirit sent from hell itself, and it must be extinguished before it does even more evil.'

'Evil?' Thomas echoed. 'What evil has the poor girl done, pray tell? She is nothing but a young maid who keeps to herself.'

'She is a wicked siren who bewitched Father Wickstanner, whose poor mortal remains even now lie within, and whose soul will not rest while the satanic influence responsible for his tragic end still walks this earth.'

'Nonsense!' Thomas exploded. 'Wickstanner was a weak fool and a drinker, though he hid that from most eyes, to be sure. The man has made a fool of himself over other young wenches, some not even grown to full womanhood and young enough to be his daughters. Perhaps he finally came to what little senses he had left when he saw what wickedness his own corruption had brought about, and if Matilda Pennywise is, or was in any way, responsible for that, then I'm sure the good Lord will thank her for it rather than punish her.'

'Blasphemy!' Crawley hissed. 'You presume to judge the Lord God's actions? Have a care, sir, or perhaps it'll not be only the witch's body that swings tonight.'

Thomas's top lip curled back. 'Have a care yourself, Master Crawley,' he growled. 'These poor fools might just let you get away with choking the life from a girl they hardly know, but I think you might find yourself faced with a cat of a different colour should you choose to try the same thing with me. Now, I'm no lawyer, but I do know that every prisoner has the right to proper representation, and from what I hear, Matilda Pennywise has had none. Indeed, you have dragged the poor creature naked in public, whipped her and abused her, and she is rendered unable even to protest her own case.'

'She is rendered unable to utter the devil curses that her kind use in order to frighten decent folk from telling the truth,' Crawley retorted. 'She has been scourged in order to try to drive the devilment from her, but the possession holds firm still. As for representation, this is no civil matter but a court of God, and the Lord himself represents all his flock, even the lambs who stray.'

'Bollocks!' Thomas spat. 'If there is evil about, then I think it comes not from the poor child. Stand aside and let me see her.'

'No,' Crawley said simply. He stood squarely in front of Handiwell, and although he was a good few years older, and looked from his features as if life had not treated him too gently, Thomas could see his lean body was well muscled. Any attempt to force a way past him would produce only an ungainly struggle and ultimate defeat under the weight of the numbers on his side. 'No,' Crawley repeated again. 'The sentence has been passed and there is no appeal, save for her soul when it comes before its Maker. Take one more step, and these fellows will cut you down, and then I *shall* charge you and you will have your own rope, no matter how many friends you may think you have here. You may turn from the church, Master Handiwell, but that does not mean everyone will do the same if you commit a heresy here!'

Some four miles further across the wooded estate, and totally oblivious to the mounting level of activity elsewhere in the forest, Sarah was only beginning to discover the depths of Ross's fertile and darkly inventive mind. Having waited while she dutifully licked clean his still erect member, he finally proceeded to the next stage of his plan to completely subjugate her, even though it was obvious she was on the verge of collapse.

Grasping her by the leather collar he had placed about her neck, he half dragged her across to the other end of the room where a round post was set into the floor and stretched up into the roof where it was attached to one of the beams. About this post, at approximately waist level, sat a circular metal collar from which projected a short horizontal metal rod, and from that rod rose a phallus so lifelike it seemed impossible it had been carved from wood, its shining surface polished until it gleamed.

In front of the post had been placed a low box. Up onto this box Sarah was now made to stand, her legs parted, while Ross loosened the handle that kept her collar tight and adjusted its height so the tip of the wooden dildo was level with her gaping pink sex.

'Get forward,' he said tersely. 'Get forward and then bend your knees as I tell you. See the nice gift I have for you?'

An hour or so earlier, Sarah knew there was no way she would have so easily conceded to the inevitable and impaled herself on the thick shaft. A day earlier and it would most certainly not have entered her so easily. She sunk down, bending her knees with a groan that became a protracted sigh, until its full length was inside her.

'Place your arms about the pole and hold yourself steady,' Ross instructed her.

Sarah reached around the wooden post, and when she realised what he intended, she clung to it fiercely as the box was dragged out from beneath her, leaving her with her toes barely touching the floor. And as the pole itself was far too small to afford her any real purchase, she had no way now of freeing herself from her impaled state.

Satisfied that the height of the collar was indeed right, Ross now proceeded to complete her predicament. From the bench he took up what Sarah at first thought was a length of wood through which two holes had been cut. But as he brought it closer, she saw it was actually two pieces of timber hinged at one end in the manner of the top section of a pillory, and similarly locked by means of a simple metal peg mechanism. Ross quickly swung the two halves open, and moving behind the post seized Sarah's wrists and placed them into the two openings, shutting the upper section and fastening it so her hands were now held some six or seven inches apart. This ensured that, while she could not fall backwards, she no longer had even the option of trying to grasp the post to lift her weight up.

Grinning, Ross walked around behind her and dealt her a hefty slap across her bare buttocks.

She jumped instinctively, and immediately felt the shaft slide out of her body and then in again, triggering a small spasm she knew only too well could easily become something more.

With a chuckle, her tormentor stepped back. 'Not yet, my little slave pet princess,' he said quietly. 'First we let you mellow a little, and then we make you dance properly. In the meantime, I think I shall reward myself with a glass or two of wine.'

'The man is a complete charlatan, Captain Hart,' Thomas Handiwell snapped. 'He is a fraud, a cheat, a thief, and now he'll be a murderer, if he isn't one already.'

'What of the fellow he claims was found dead in the woods?' Timothy Hart asked. His pale eyes were watery from lack of sleep, and he had hoped to use the time before his messenger returned from Portsmouth to rest, but the innkeeper seemed determined to keep him from his bed.

'A stranger to these parts,' Handiwell said. 'He arrived here with Crawley, so no one knows anything of him saving he looked as rough as the second man and he's probably no good, like his damned master.'

'And the evidence against the grandmother concerning his death?'

'Evidence?' Thomas slammed a fist onto the bar top with such force that two empty flagons at the far end bounced and rattled. 'There's no damned evidence at all, saving that two of his new *converts* are apparently prepared to swear they saw the old woman and young James Calthorpe near the hut in which the body was discovered. 'Tis as flimsy a case as they have against the girl.'

'And yet they intend to hang her on that,' Hart pointed out.

'Not if you stop them. Your uniform should carry the weight that my reputation apparently does not.'

'My uniform has no jurisdiction over matters of the cloth,' Hart said. 'My presence here is tenuous at best, in any case, and I dare not try to interfere with the church.'

'The church,' Thomas growled. 'The damned church has much to answer for, in my opinion. For God's sake, man, can't you see this is a crock of shit? Surely you could declare martial law, or something, *anything* that will delay this so-called execution until we can bring the facts before a proper authority.'

Hart shook his head. 'I should need authority from higher up for anything like that,' he said firmly. 'Why, I could not, dare not, even pursue one of your highwaymen into that church if he sought sanctuary there. It is the law, Master Handiwell.'

'Then the law should be kicked in the arse,' Thomas retorted, 'and all its so called guardians with it!'

Isobel moved with great care now, walking very slowly in order to prevent the hated bells from bouncing, and ducking behind trees and bushes every few yards in order to listen, as well as the leather of the bird helmet permitted. Twice already she had thought herself discovered, and spun around at sudden noises that, thankfully, turned out to be only birds taking to the air, no doubt as startled by her presence as she was by theirs.

Crouching in a hollow amidst several tangled bushes and brambles, she began to wonder if her best bet might now be to remain where she was and wait out whatever remained of her hour. At least half of it must have elapsed by now, for she had travelled the better part of two miles, she was sure of that. She had even come upon the eastern perimeter fence once and followed it for a few minutes before turning back to the cover of the trees.

Her present hiding place was as good as any she had so far considered. She was still within a hundred yards or so of the boundary, but far enough away from the cleared space that followed it around the perimeter not to risk running into the regular fence patrols. The men who guarded the fence were not part of the hunt, but they would also have no way of knowing she was not just another slave up for sport. There had been more than one occasion when a girl had fallen into their clutches and been roughly used before being turned back into the game.

Damn Bressingham, damn Roddy and damn her own arrogance and foolish impetuosity. This was not turning out to be the adventure she had believed it would be. The heavy boots drained all the strength from her leg muscles, and the two dildos kept up their malign work, so that despite her efforts to the contrary her body remained on the brink of total surrender. Her nipples throbbed in the grip of the weighted clamps and all she wanted was for the tower bell to sound so she could make her way back to the house, claim her victory, and have the maids fill a tub for her.

After she had soaked away all her aches and pains she would find a way to get back at that bastard, Roddy, for she knew he still desired her body and the things she could do for him that surely those two little black bitches could not...

Sarah started to pray, but the words became a jumble in her head and the dagger-spasms now wracking her calves and shoulders made any hope of recovering her powers of concentration quite forlorn. Poised almost on tiptoe for several minutes after Ross left her, she soon realised that maintaining this position for long would be impossible. And so, reluctantly, she allowed her weight to slowly subside until the projecting dildo was fully buried inside her, the horizontal support pressing up between the lips of her sex.

It was far from comfortable, but at least she was now able to lift her legs and move her feet about in an effort to ease her tortured muscles, although even that small amount of movement resulted in all sorts of unwanted and shameful pulsing sensations. Gagged again, she could not protest, and despite knowing that Ross's return would simply herald another round of painful humiliation, she found herself wishing for the sound of his boots in the passageway.

Nothing, she told herself fiercely, fighting to keep the tattered remnants of both her pride and her sanity intact, could be worse than what she had suffered at the beast's hands already. Being left as she was now, quite unable to do anything to ease her suffering, the oppressive silence broken only by the occasional birdsong from outside, was in many ways far worse.

At last she heard him returning. He was whistling quietly to himself, a melody she vaguely recalled but could not name, and when he strode into the room and around in front of her, she saw that he looked quite pleased with himself. To judge by the flush in his cheeks, he had taken more than just a couple of glasses of wine while he was away.

'Ah, my sweet little slave pet,' he crooned, pursing his lips in a mocking kiss. 'So glad to see you're still here and that no harm's come to you. I hope you have not been too bored in my absence, but I do find that giving a girl time to reflect every now and then is so very beneficial to her future conduct.' He began pacing slowly around her in a circle, studying her carefully from every angle and occasionally reaching out to stroke her shoulder, her thigh, her stomach, her breast, the nape of her neck. His gentle caresses were at odds with his earlier treatment of her, but they steadily began to arouse the same sort of sensations.

Sarah whimpered quietly and arched her back as she fought to resist what she was feeling.

'Yes, such excellent raw material,' he smirked, running the backs of two fingers over her left breast, pausing only to squeeze the very tip of her nipple gently between them. 'You see what the right training can achieve, my pet? A

64

day or two more and you'll be just perfect, worthy of double the price you might have fetched when you first arrived. A week from now, and it will seem unnatural for you not to be filled with one cock or another, be it made of flesh-and-blood, wood or leather. The lust lies within every female, it just needs the right person to find it and allow it to bloom. It is like exorcising a devil, or maybe that should be *exercising* a devil, freeing the bonds of the spirit.'

Sarah eyed him sullenly, hating him for the fact that his words, although slurred and obviously the product of a demented mind, nevertheless rang all too true in some ways. Was it really so easy for one human being to manipulate, and eventually rule, another by these means? Could she really be reduced to how she felt now, let alone become the sort of creature he was describing and predicting he would make her?

'Time for a little dancing class, I think.'

Sarah grunted and tried to ease the pressure in her crotch, once more taking as much weight as she could onto her toes.

Ross patted her across the buttocks, chuckling. 'Such a fine body,' he said. 'A little fleshy in places, but then so many young women do not exercise properly. A week or so here usually takes care of such things. Yes, indeed,' he continued, moving towards the bench, 'the right food, the proper exercise and training, and you won't recognise your old self by the time you're ready to leave here.'

The sound of jingling bells warned Matilda of approaching danger just in time. She had just ducked into the bushes when the bird-girl burst out of the woods on the far side of the little clearing, her breasts bouncing, her winged arms flapping wildly at her sides. Her pursuer must have been close, for as she ran the poor creature kept trying to look back over her shoulder, and this inevitably hastened her downfall.

Halfway across the grassy area she stumbled, and before she could even attempt to steady herself she was flying headlong. She landed with a sickening thump that must have driven the air from her lungs, for aside from a muffled groan, she gave no cry of pain.

A moment later her nemesis appeared. Like the other hunters he was masked and dressed in black, so who he was Matilda could not tell, although his slight paunch suggested he was neither Roderick Grayling nor Guy Bressingham. She also surmised that the fallen bird-girl could not be the stupid creature who had actually volunteered herself for this insane hunt. No, it wasn't that silly Isobel creature, for this girl had no ribbon between her breast rings.

The black-garbed hunter, seeing his quarry fallen and motionless, slowed to a walk, and with an effort not to appear as out of breath as he plainly was, he sauntered easily over to where she lay. He stood over her, a smirk spreading across the lower half of his face. He looked down at his prey, and then turned her over onto her back with the tip of his boot.

The girl's eyes were open; she was conscious, if all but paralysed from the sickening fall, and Matilda could almost taste the fear she must now be experiencing.

The hunter bent slightly at the waist and said, 'A brave effort, my little peacock. That was a fine chase back there. Now then, shall we have you up?' He reached down and grasped her by the shoulders, pulling her limp form into a sitting position. Breathing heavily from the added exertion, he crouched down beside her. He was obviously not accustomed to so much physical exercise, Matilda realised, but she also knew this would not stop him from enjoying his prize once he got his breath back.

Sure enough, after about a minute or so, he stood up again and commanded the girl to do the same. Her lungs now working normally once more, she did as he instructed and stood with her head lowered, her arms limp at her sides, in an attitude of defeat and surrender. The man then reached out and flicked each of her nipple bells before walking around and dropping to one knee behind her, where he began fumbling with the buckle of the strap holding the leather phalluses in place.

'We'll just test the meat for tenderness, I think,' he said. 'No point in bringing a tough bird to the table, so a little preliminary tenderising seems to be just the thing.'

The multi-thonged whip Ross selected from amongst the implements on the bench was much larger, heavier, and altogether more ominous than the miniature implement he used on Sarah earlier, and a cold knot began to form in the pit of her stomach as she eyed it.

'My *dancing tutor*, my pet,' he informed her, 'or should I say *your* dancing tutor.' Without further warning, he flicked out the tails so they snaked through the air to wrap themselves across the top of her buttocks.

As the first searing pain shot through her she found herself leaping into the air, although not so far as to be able to detach herself from the shaft impaling her. And before she had time to consider and react, she slammed down again, driving the polished wooden shaft deep into her cleft. Her scream of pain contorted itself into another cry that was at once terror, agony, and something purely animalistic.

Again the whip cracked, and although she tried to anticipate the blow, all she succeeded in doing this time was moderating her overall reaction. The wooden strut into which her wrists had been locked rasped up and down the pole as her feet shot into the air, splaying open on either side of the post as she kicked out wildly, fighting to overcome the myriad sensations battling inside her.

The third time the whip coiled about her shoulders, its effect was to send her legs back downwards, the balls of her feet and her toes scrabbling for purchase as her upper body jerked forward until brought up short by the main timber. Tears streaming from her eyes and fires welling up inside, she bit hard into the gag and tensed for the next onslaught, but Ross had further refinements he was about to subject her to.

Tucking the handle of the whip into his belt, he strode back to the bench yet again, and this time he returned with a device that left Sarah completely cold and uncomprehending. It comprised a short, stubby phallus made of some kind of dark wood attached to a broad leather strap, and she did not see any way in which it could be employed, for it was surely too fat in its girth to fit into her one remaining lower orifice. However, as Ross began to fasten the strap about the pole before her face, she saw two thinner straps dangling from it and finally understood its purpose. Up close, she saw that the dildo was covered with a highly polished leather skin, the surface of which was scarred with teeth marks.

'We must learn poise as well as the correct dance steps,' Ross chided her mockingly, 'and poise requires that the head remain steady at all times.' Having satisfied himself that the gag was well anchored, he quickly removed the one already in her mouth and tossed it over onto the bench. 'Now then,' he said quietly, 'let me see you take to this cock as you did to mine earlier.'

'Oh please, no...' Sarah began, but the look in his eyes, and the complete lack of emotion on his face, told she was wasting her time begging.

He nodded curtly. 'Take it in,' he said, 'and let's see your pretty mouth stretch for it.'

And stretch Sarah's mouth did, for the girth of the hideous gag was far greater than any human counterpart could ever be. Thankfully, however, it was also much shorter than the usual flesh-and- blood equivalent, or else as Ross tightened the straps about her neck to prevent her expelling the foul monster she would surely have choked on it. As it was, her jaw felt it must surely come unhinged, and her cheeks bulged as the saliva began to trickle out onto her chin.

'Now,' Ross said, taking out the whip again, 'let's see you dance and hear you hum the tune, shall we?'

Jane had to work hard to keep Oona in check, for the dog-girl was eager to get properly into the hunt and did not seem to understand why this woman who held her leash kept hauling her back on it every time she tried to surge forward. Jane, however, knew exactly what she was doing, and exactly where she wanted to be. When the pair finally came out onto what the Grayling people always called the top path, which ran parallel to the northern boundary fence, she was certain they had arrived well ahead of their quarry.

'Settle now, Oona,' she hissed, and tugged sharply on the leash.

Oona looked back at her, and at the cane she brandished, and gave a low growling moan.

Jane tugged again and indicated for the dog-girl to return to her side by slapping the cane against her boot. 'You'll get your fill of warm pussy soon enough, you horny little wretch. So why waste your strength chasing the game when the game will come to us? Now, let's see where the best place is to wait up, shall we?' She had already worked out that there were two options when it came to laying an ambush for the hapless fugitive, and as she studied the remains of two old fallen oaks, Jane decided the second choice would be the best. She chose a thick clump of evergreen bushes that had pushed out until they narrowed the path to almost a quarter of its width. There was no need even to make an effort to hide, all they had to do was step back behind the screen of foliage and wait until they heard the girl approaching. All Jane had to decide now was whether to shoot the girl in the thigh at point-blank range, or whether to let Oona loose and let her bring the bird down in full flight.

She opted for the latter. The running girl would be exhausted by the time she reached this point, and Oona would be even more frustrated if she was not permitted to do what she had been trained for. Besides, Jane thought with a grin, Oona at the run was an impressive spectacle, and the creature would enjoy her rewards the better for having been the one to make the catch.

'Quiet now, you silly bitch!' Jane hissed. 'The pretty birdie will be along very shortly and we don't want to scare her away into the bushes.'

Men, Harriet knew, both from stories her father had told her and from accounts she read in books in the library room at Barten Meade, were capable of stooping to unimaginable depths of wickedness. But she had also been brought up to believe that no matter how dreadful and hopeless a situation might seem that good always triumphed over evil in the end.

Huddled naked and alone in the corner of the crypt chamber, she realised how naive such a belief was. Until now, she had done nothing that would be deemed so terribly wrong in the eyes of her Maker. True, she had from time to time looked upon her reflection in the mirror and taken pride in her fine features, her soft eyes and beautiful hair, but then what girl wouldn't, she thought fiercely. Was that a justification for the fact that she now had no hair, that her beautiful face had been hidden inside this tight and dank-smelling mask and that her body was now covered in welts? Her virginity, the purity she had cherished for so long, had been stripped from her as brutally as had been her clothes. She had been whipped and called names no Christian maiden should ever hear, and why?

Jane Handiwell, and her father's affection for Harriet. It was an affection Harriet had never encouraged or cultivated even though he was as straightforward, steadfast and uncorrupted as it was possible for any man to be. Yet he had unknowingly nurtured an evil viper in the bosom of his home, a daughter who repaid his love and affection with spite and treachery.

Such a good man was Thomas, Harriet knew, that he would not for one instant believe his beloved daughter could even think of harming anyone he cherished. So honest was he that he would be staggered beyond belief to learn that his little Jane could even think he would allow his love for another to come between them. He would not be able to believe his daughter capable of such wicked jealousy, nor of turning from the honest path he himself had trod all his life.

Even now he would be out there somewhere searching for Harriet, but he would be searching in completely the wrong place, suspecting all the wrong people. Whatever was happening at Grayling Hall, and Jane was doubtless involved in that, Thomas would not find her there, and neither would he think of looking closer to home. Even Crawley had no idea she was not Matilda, and the foul beasts now in his pay were just as ignorant; to them she was simply a welcome distraction, a *something* rather than a someone. They could use her to slake their lust before the hangman's rope put an end to her suffering.

Harriet bowed her head, closing her eyes to fight back tears imagining the scene after they cut down her dead body, stripped away the terrible bridle and mask, and revealed her true identity. She prayed Thomas would not be there when the moment came, for she could imagine the guilt he would feel and how he would berate himself for not realising she had been so close all along. He would doubtless shed tears, beat his breast, and possibly even try to avenge her death. He would perhaps even forfeit his own life in doing so, for there would be those who would seek to protect the vile witchfinder and his perverted view of religion. But what was even worse was that Thomas Handiwell would probably, almost certainly, never know that the person most guilty for all of this was his own daughter.

The fleeing bird-girl really had no chance. The clinking of her nipple bells heralded her approach, so Jane was able to stand and listen long enough to determine that her prey was moving at a fast walk. Oona began growling as he picked up the sounds and the scent, but a sharp tap from the cane silenced her.

'Wait!' Jane commanded in a fierce whisper. 'Let's at least make some sport of this!'

Oona gave a final whimper and then crouched tensely, the firm muscles of her buttocks twitching as Jane grasped her collar firmly to make sure she could not move until the precise moment.

A second or two later the bird-girl came into view only a few yards away, but she was looking neither to left nor right; she was ambling along with a laboured, rolling gait, panting noisily, clearly struggling.

Jane made a face, a look of disappointment, for she had wanted her prey tired, but this one looked to be on the verge of collapse. 'Well,' she whispered, her mouth close to Oona's ear, 'let's see if the bird bitch has anything left in her, shall we?' She stood upright again and yelled at the top of her voice, 'Ho-la! Ho-la! Ho, there!'

The sudden shout totally startled the girl. She stumbled, jerking her head around in the direction of the challenge. Her eyes widening in horror when she saw both the black-garbed Jane and the bristling dog-girl, she took off with renewed vigour.

'That's more like it!' Jane cried triumphantly. Oona pulled hard on the leash and all but toppled her, forcing her to use the cane to check her. 'Wait,' she shrieked. 'Give her a sporting start first. You'll have her down in no time.'

Jane waited until the fleeing mass of flapping feathers had gained about thirty yards before she released her human hound with a cry of encouragement. Oona needed no urging and was off in a flash, running with a loping stride that ate up the ground between herself and her prey at an astonishing rate.

The girl, hearing her nemesis closing upon her, looked back once, her eyes round with terror and desperation, and Jane, who was now trotting along in their wake, saw that she did indeed manage to accelerate just a little, but not enough, and it was far too late. Oona suddenly leapt, stretching out horizontally, her clawed hands grasping. The girl gave a shriek of pain as the sharp metal scraped down her thighs, and then she fell, tumbling over and over with a snarling Oona wrestling and kicking her down.

For a few more seconds the poor wench tried to put up a fight, but then she plainly realised it was a completely unequal struggle, and rolling over onto her stomach, she lay still. Oona perched on her back in an attitude of triumph, her claws settling into her victim's shoulders in case she should decide to try another escape.

'Well done, Oona, you beautiful bitch.' Jane ran up alongside her. 'A shame she didn't give you more of a run, but I daresay there will be a chance for you to catch another bird before this afternoon is over.' She reached into the small pouch at her belt and drew out a coil of thin twine. 'We'll just truss her ready for the stuffing at table and leave her for the grooms to collect later.' Oona let out a plaintive whine. 'But not before you have her for stuffing yourself,' Jane added, smiling. She stepped back and flicked the ground with the tip of her cane. 'Go to it then,' she urged, 'see her off, you wicked bitch- dog.'

Oona crawled from the prone figure and deftly flipped her onto her back. The girl was conscious and aware enough, but all the fight had gone out of her and even the sight of Oona's member beginning to appear from between her nether lips did no more than bring a strangled gasp from behind her gag.

'Here, girl,' Jane said, stooping beside Oona. She reached beneath her and took the steadily thickening shaft in her gloved hand, masturbating it gently, something she would never have done with a normal man's organ. Oona let out a curious purring growl and began to pant. 'Now then,' Jane said, feeling the full hardness in her fingers, 'I should say you're near enough ready, so I'll just take this strap out of your way and you can fill her to your little black doggie-heart's content.'

Sarah had guessed Ross's intentions from the way in which he secured her on the thick shaft, but she was totally unprepared for the way in which her body reacted to the stimulation caused by the way she bucked and writhed beneath the slow, steady whipping. With the phallic gag preventing her from moving her head and neck, her instinctive reaction to each stroke was to arch her back in and out, an exercise which lifted her weight, and then down again, so that now she rode the dildo in rhythm with his lashes.

Whack! The leather tails coiled about her protruding buttocks and thighs, and her feet flailed hopelessly just above the ground as another howl of pain, mixed with an insidious, unbidden pleasure, forced its way past her distorted lips.

Whack! The braids stung her calf muscles, sending her legs shooting outwards. The board that held her wrists slid up and down the pole as she fought to try to regain control of herself, but it was already a lost battle.

'Dance, my pretty pet,' Ross bellowed. 'Dance like a butterfly and show your master just what a brazen little slave slut you're becoming.'

Whack! The leather slapped across her shoulders. Unable to see clearly beyond a red mist in which danced a myriad of startling lights, Sarah screamed through her gag and surrendered to the unreal world clutching at her. The pain vanished into the strange ether in which she swam, and was replaced by a burning fire of passion and desire that drove her on through a grotesque ballet she performed like a helpless marionette. She knew nothing, felt nothing and cared for nothing save filling the inhuman hunger boiling up inside her from mysterious depths of her flesh she had never even suspected existed.

The terrible wailing sound they had first heard about a hundred yards back in the woods was much louder now, and as he peered through the bushes, Paddy Riley realised it was coming from inside the timbered building that stood in the centre of the small clearing before them. Behind him, there was a rustling and cracking of dry twigs as Sean Kelly wriggled up to join him.

'Will you listen to that?' Kelly gasped. 'Have you ever heard the likes of that before? Sounds like someone's torturing some poor bloody animal to death in there!' As he spoke they heard the sharp thwack of a whiplash, and the keening wail rose to a new crescendo.

'Animal my balls,' Paddy grunted. 'Ain't no animal in there, saving you mean a human one.'

'Never could it be,' Kelly hissed. 'No human could be making a racket of that kind.'

'I tell you it is,' Paddy persisted. 'That's some poor female making the devil's own, and taking it too.' The crack of the whip cut through the still afternoon air again. The howling rose in pitch and hung as if suspended above the trees.

'What are we going to do?' Kelly demanded. His face had taken on a grey pallor and his knuckles were white from how fiercely he was gripping the stock of his musket. The howl ebbed and flowed, becoming a choking sob that was again followed by another crack of the whip, and a renewed shrieking that threatened to make them all sick to their stomachs.

Paddy sighed and reached for the long knife he always carried slung from his belt. 'Do?' he echoed, his voice sounding dull, almost inhuman. 'There's only one thing we *can* do, unless you think we can just sit here listening to that, or just up and walk away.'

Crouched down in the centre of a circle of bushes, Isobel was beginning to doubt her senses. Time seemed to have stopped, for she was sure the hour must have elapsed by now and yet there was still no sound from the bell-tower bell. The slightest sound, muffled by the soft leather of the helmet pressing against her ears, sent her heart leaping into her throat as she feared imminent discovery, but each time she realised it was only a bird, or a small animal scurrying through the undergrowth.

The sound of her breathing seemed magnified tenfold, the pounding of her heart an ominous echo, and her smallest movement seemed to set off a cacophony of bells that she was convinced could be heard for miles around. In her head pictures swirled around in a kaleidoscope of bared teeth and brown arms tipped with glittering claws surrounded by grinning faces, Roderick Grayling's and Guy Bressingham's mocking visages glorying in her failure.

Isobel shook her head. This was foolishness, she told herself firmly. She had gone to ground some time since, and she was as far away from the likely hunting area as it was possible to be without actually venturing towards the cleared areas along the perimeter of the fence. She was also well hidden; six or seven feet of thick foliage surrounded her on all sides, thoroughly screening her from anyone passing within even a few paces of her hiding place.

She eased herself slowly around into a sitting position, taking great care to ensure that her breasts did not bounce with the movement, trying to reassure herself that it could now only be a matter of minutes before her wager was won. She peered down at the bright ribbon between her nipple rings. It had to be Bressingham who caught her, which must surely have tipped the odds heavily in her favour. Perhaps, she reflected, she should have cut westwards and crossed into the territory where the other bird-girls were being hunted; that might well have confused the issue considerably and left Bressingham scouring a totally empty section of the forest.

It was too late now, however, and she must surely be within touching distance of victory. She held her breath and willed her heart to beat silently as she closed her eyes to concentrate on listening...

The afternoon breeze had picked up, the leaves rustling gently beneath a wind blowing from several different directions, and she could hear birds as they chirped away. Apart from that, there was nothing but silence... a silence suddenly punctuated by the mournful and toneless tolling of a bell that sent a shiver of fear through her until she realised what it meant. Her heart leapt as she jumped to her feet, and but for the gag in her mouth she would have cried out in triumph.

She had won! The hour was up, and she was still free! Bressingham had failed and she could now return to the house in triumph and collect her money from all those who had looked upon her so mockingly as she was led out and herded together with the other bird-girls.

With a deep sigh of relief, Isobel stooped again and began to push her way through the tangle of branches, not caring that they dragged the feathers from her bedraggled wings. She was already counting her winnings and rehearsing the way in which she would verbally repay all those fools for ever doubting her.

The sight that greeted the two troopers as they entered the last chamber inside the barn brought them up with a shock. Only the fact that the man with the whip was wielding it with so much concentrated attention allowed them the extra seconds they needed to recover their composure, and to leap upon him before he had time to register their presence. As Sean Kelly took him into a fierce body hug, Paddy drove the butt of his musket into the pit of the fellow's stomach, driving the breath out of him, and then clubbed him unconscious with another fierce blow to the side of his head.

To their further astonishment, the naked girl clinging to the post continued to let out a high-pitched wail, and all the while her body jerked up and down, her breasts bouncing and her legs flailing. For a moment none of the men realised what was happening. It was Sean who finally saw the projecting stud and its vertical extension, or at least the small part of it not embedded within her.

'Mother of God!' he breathed, and quickly crossed himself. 'The lass is friggin' a bloody pole!'

'Just grab her shoulders,' Paddy snapped, promptly stepping forward. 'Hold her tight and I'll get a hold under her. If she keeps this up she'll do herself some harm.'

However, once he had unfastened the straps holding her mouth open around the gag, the only danger of harm came from the girl's wild kicking. Even when they had finally managed to lift her clear of the pole, she continued to writhe in their grasp like a demented serpent. Only the fact that her wrists were still held firm inside the miniature pillory bar prevented her from doing them some real damage. And then, abruptly, her fit subsided, and with a despairing groan she sagged in their arms, her knees buckling. At this, Paddy promptly transferred his attention to freeing her arms. Quickly finding and working out the simple locking mechanism, he opened the bar. They then carried her clear of the post and laid her across the hard earth floor as gently as her twitching and jerking permitted. Looking up, Paddy saw young Toby Blaine standing in the doorway, his eyes wide.

'Go on, lad,' he snapped. 'This is no place for you. Get yourself to the outer door and keep watch. This blackguard may well have friends close by and we don't want to give them the jump on us. Here,' he urged, seeing Toby's lack of response, 'take my pistol. You know how to use it?'

Dumbly, Toby nodded.

'Good lad. And aim at the body; it's a bigger target than the head. Now, Sean lad, you hold her still and let's see what all this is about. This strapping about her middle can't be doing her any good.' Sean, he could see, was only marginally less shocked by the scene they had witnessed than the boy, and seemed almost afraid to touch the naked girl.

'Will you keep a decent hold on her?' he asked impatiently. 'This is no time for trying to play the bloody gentleman. And try not to let her poor back rub on the floor, either; her flesh is sore as hell from the look of it.'

'I don't like this at all, Paddy,' Sean whispered. 'She acts as if she's possessed by the devil himself.'

'Pa!' He aimed a half-hearted slap at Sean's head. 'The only thing as has possessed this one is that bloody cock thing up there.' He nodded tersely back at the object of her degradation. 'Your man had her bouncing up and down on the damned thing for the Lord knows how long, and she lost her mind to lust, that's all.'

'Is she going to die, do you think?'

Paddy peered down at the girl's face. Her eyes were closed and her mouth open. 'Well,' he said slowly, 'I've never heard of a body dying from a good shagging, but then this is something else again, Sean, and I'm no doctor. But no, I think she'll be all right in a while. This is just a fit of the hysterics and it'll pass, like everything else, in time.'

It had felt like an eternity. It had been the longest hour in Isobel's life. But now, as she stumbled wearily but triumphantly out onto the path, it was over and she had won. She stopped to look up at the sky and draw a deep breath in through her nostrils. The air tasted fresh and good, apart from the faint aroma of the leather still encasing her head and face. She grinned around the disfiguring gag and groaned with anticipation. The hood, the feathers, the gag, *everything* would soon be in the past and she would enjoy every moment of Bressingham's defeat.

She pulled back her shoulders and thrust her breasts forward in a defiant attitude, jiggling them slightly so the bells tinkled merrily, but now the tiny ringing sounds were peals of victory; gone was their haunting mockery. Yes, she thought, this was the way to return, not cowering helplessly but rather glorying in her victory, proudly displaying her body... and suddenly her muscles contracted and went into spasms as the two shafts inside her reminded of their presence. She shuddered, started to fight their wicked influence, and then shook her head. Why fight it? She had already won.

She fell to her knees, bowing her feathered head, and her body began to convulse as waves of unbelievable power and release swept through her.

She did not notice the bright length of ribbon fluttering innocently on the end of the bramble branch behind her, where it had caught and been tugged free of the loose knots Grayling had tied in his eagerness to begin the hunt. She did not notice that the ribbon no longer hung between her clamped and distended nipples as she surrendered to the power of her orgasm. She did not notice the two pairs of eyes that watched her from deep in the trees, one pair with a mixture of disdain and amusement, the other with a ferocious hunger even the brown furry mask could not hide.

Crawley stood silhouetted in the doorway by the light of a lamp behind him, and there were other men out in the passageway. 'Prepare her with another scourging,' he said, 'then wash her down with salted water and bring her to the rear door. She shall stand at the stake and watch Wickstanner laid to rest, and then the sun dipping towards the hills for the last time. The whole village shall then see what becomes of those who dare to meddle in the ways of the dark side.'

'You want that we should remove the hood and the other thing?' a male voice asked.

For a moment Harriet's hopes rose. If Crawley's henchmen knew her true identity they would be unlikely to help him kill her, even though the man himself might want to do so in an effort to cover up his mistake.

'No.' Harriet's heart sank once more. 'No,' Crawley repeated, 'we'll not risk giving her any chance to spin her enchantments again. You all saw what happened to Father Wickstanner. No, leave the witch to her silence and prepare her as I said.' He turned away, and his place was taken by several other shadows before the one carrying the lantern entered the little chamber, flooding it with a light that, though dim in reality, seemed as bright as the sun to Harriet after her hours of near darkness.

'Aye,' said Thaddeus Gilbert, looming over her, 'we'll prepare the witch with one last good tupping from us all, eh lads?'

'Well then, Paddy,' Sean Kelly sighed and leaned back against the post that had until so recently been the host to Sarah's humiliating surrender, 'you're the sergeant, so what do we do next?'

Paddy Riley, still crouching by the semiconscious form on the floor, looked up with a grimace. 'If there's one thing I'm sure of in all this, Sean me boy,' he said softly, 'it's that I'm sure of nothing. I've never come across the likes of any of this in all my days, and if I never come across it again, it'll be a day too soon.'

'Any idea who she is?' Sean asked. 'Not the one we came for, I'd guess, or the lad would've said.'

'It doesn't matter who the poor lass is,' Paddy muttered. 'Wherever she came from, and whoever she is, she sure as heaven's mercy doesn't want to be staying here a minute longer than she has to.'

'Amen to that,' Sean agreed. 'But how do we get her out of here? We could try carrying her, but that leaves us with only one gun, unless we count young Toby out there, and I'd not like to leave the state of my hide in the hands of a whelp.'

'I'm trying to think,' Paddy muttered, sitting back on his haunches and running a hand over his rough chin. 'You're right, of course, we can't carry her, and I don't like to beat a retreat without at least trying to find out if the other woman is somewhere hereabouts.'

'Maybe we could risk leaving her here for a bit?' Sean suggested. 'Yon fella there looks out of it for a good while yet, if he ever does come round again. We could leave the lad to watch over the pair of them, and give him that length of timber with instructions to whack the bastard again if he so much as stirs.'

'And then who's going to tell us if and when we find Mistress Harriet?' Paddy shook his head. 'No, we'll need to be a bit cleverer than that, Sean Kelly, and I have the scrapings of an idea.'

'You said that a while back,' Sean reminded him.

Paddy nodded. 'I know I did,' he conceded, 'and that plan may still hold good.' He stood up again. 'We'll have to leave Toby with the girl for a while, yes, but only for as long as it takes us to grab one of those black-hooded bastards out there. If we can grab two, all the better, but one will do. Then we'll need to see where they keep their horses, and with luck a coach or a wagon.'

'And then we look for the other girl?'

'Maybe,' Paddy replied, 'and maybe not. Seems they have the girls here running about in all sorts of garb, and even this one has been shaved. Young Toby might not recognise our lady, but I know who he *would* recognise.'

'And who might that be?'

Paddy pursed his lips and walked slowly towards the doorway. 'Sean,' he said slowly, 'there's two ways to win a battle and I've seen both. There's the one where the generals say "charge up that hill lads and take the flag and don't worry how many of you all get cut to ribbons by the cannons and muskets, 'cause it's for king and country you're fighting". Of course,' he added wryly, 'now it's for Cromwell and country, but it amounts to the same thing: you end up just as dead if you get a ball through the heart. And then,' he continued, turning back to stare at the girl who was now moaning softly and rolling her head slowly from side to side, 'there's the other way, where a couple of worthy lads sneak up around the side and climb the hill from the back. They grab the flag, shoot the enemy officers, and then grab the main general as a hostage.'

'You've seen that done?' Sean asked, visibly impressed.

Paddy kept a straight face for a second or two, and then his weathered features wrinkled into a broad grin. 'Well, maybe not quite the way I just told it,' he confessed, 'but it always seemed to me it would be a damned sight less wasteful if it could be done, and there's been a war or two won by ways not so very different. When Cromwell grabbed the old king there were still thousands of royalists ready to fight, but did they? No, they all laid down their guns and went home like good little boys.'

'I don't get you,' Sean said.

Paddy smirked at him. 'No,' he said, 'I know you don't. But then, like you said, I'm the sergeant, ain't I?'

'Wait, Oona,' Jane whispered, bending close to the dog-girl's furry head. 'Wait just a little while now and you shall have your sport. Let the stupid bitch wander a little further down the path, and then no one can say we must have seen that ribbon.'

The pair had been hiding behind the trees, yet Isobel probably would not have seen them had they strolled casually down the middle of the path; since emerging from her hiding place she had not once looked back. The tolling of the tower bell had signalled her wager won, and now it was plain enough to see she had abandoned all caution.

'But no one said anything about what was to happen after the hour,' Jane chuckled as much to herself as to Oona. 'She may have won her bet with that oaf, but no one has signalled the end of the hunt and she's still fair game as far as I can see. Besides, Bressingham's bird was marked out especially and we see no mark on this one, do we, Oona?'

Beside her, walking with her distinctive crouch, the dog-girl gave a low growl.

Jane shushed her. This was a rare chance, she thought, a rare chance to even the unfair balances of life. She had known Isobel de Lednay for a few years now, and the young aristocrat had made her disdain for the common innkeeper's daughter plain enough for all to see. Jane's presence at Grayling Hall owed everything to her childhood friendship with Ellen, and whilst Roderick himself never alluded to her roots (after all, Jane and her little gang were valuable to him) Isobel knew nothing of Jane's nocturnal double life and wasted no opportunity to score points over her.

Unfair balances were no better illustrated than in Isobel, Jane thought grimly. Born to wealth, she was also beautiful, as beautiful as any female could be, and men fawned after her, even if inside that pretty fluffy head was a fluffy brain. And here she was, still dressed in that ridiculous bird costume, still helpless with her arms trapped in the stiff wings and still with her pretty little mouth filled with the foul leather gag, her face hidden behind the feathered mask and beak. Who could possibly blame Jane, or anyone else for that matter, if they assumed she was just another of the slave girls? So far there had been no sounds of gunfire from anywhere in the woods, so it was safe to assume none of the other hunters had yet run their prey to the ground. If any had, they had done so without resorting to firing one of the numbing slugs first.

'Time for a little fun, I think,' Jane whispered. 'Our pretty bird is going to find out just what it means to be properly stuffed for the platter. And then,' she added, a malicious grin spreading across the visible part of her face, 'we'll even give her a good basting in her own juices, methinks.'

The mournful tolling of the tower bell reached Kitty as she was loping along through a long stretch of meadow near the northern perimeter fence of the Grayling estate, although in truth she had absolutely no idea where she was and cared not a jot. For her, the entire hunt scenario had now moved into the realm of sheer enjoyment. She was out and free in the fresh air and sunshine, and the two dildos were sending messages she was quite content to surrender herself to periodically.

Compared to her more recent experiences, this was as close to bliss as she could ever have hoped to be, and the fact that she knew she would ultimately be run to ground by one of the hunters held no terror for her whatsoever. She raised her arms as she ran and flapped her artificial wings, snorting past her gag with the sheer joy of a freedom she was enjoying to the full.

She was a bird, a beautiful, gaudy, brilliant and bizarre bird, a creation of men for men, and she felt so good knowing there were men running around out there somewhere whose sole purpose for the next few hours was to claim her for their prize. The feeling was almost overwhelming... so many men, so many rich and powerful men, and the one thing they all had fixed in their minds was claiming her for their own.

She staggered to a halt and leaned against a sapling, tears of laughter clouding her eyes. Oh, this was so wonderful, so totally wonderful. To think she had risen from what she had been to become an object of so much desire and admiration.

Kitty peered down at herself and at her awesome breasts, their nipples pulled and swollen with rings and bells, and she knew the power of freedom had been granted her in the form of these two huge orbs. For did not all men stare at them in wonderment and seek to have and hold them? The men here were little different from men everywhere, she concluded. Soon she would be sold again, and this time it would be her ability to please that would ensure she found a master worthy of owning her.

She tottered across to where a young tree had somehow become uprooted and was lying almost horizontally, its broken branches tangled up in a particularly thick clump of bushes so the trunk was held a few feet perpendicular to the ground. Using one winged arm to steady herself, she swung her right leg over it and settled herself astride the smooth bark. As the pressure of her weight drove the front dildo deeper inside her, Kitty let out a moan of appreciation.

She was bored with running now... no, not with the running but with the lack of anything to run from, or to. Let them find her, and meantime she would prepare in her own way. Slowly she began rocking back and forth, her weight first pressing on one dildo, and then the other...

With Oona's weight pinning her down, snarling fangs only inches from her neck and the savage metal claws digging into her unprotected flesh, Isobel offered little resistance as Jane went to work with the thin twine.

First she bent each of the hapless girl's legs double, lashing her ankles to her thighs, and then, pulling her winged arms behind her, she wrapped more twine around them, pinning them against her body. Finally she added loops from her bound legs over her shoulders and the back of her neck, and completed her task by tightening loops about her breasts so her victim was left doubled over and held immobile in the manner of a bird ready for the oven. She was truly trussed for the table, her head bowed and her buttocks thrust up into the air, the restraining strap and twin dildos removed and cast aside so her sex was left pouting open and fully exposed from behind.

'Excellent,' Jane sighed, cutting away the unwanted twine with her knife. 'Ready for plucking and equally as ready for fucking. Yes, whether for plucking or fucking, she looks delicious. Doesn't she, Oona?'

The dog-girl growled and moved around to sniff at the proffered goods, but she made no move to take advantage of the prisoner. Jane, however, was less reserved. Kneeling, she extended a gloved hand and began to caress Isobel's compressed and puckered labial lips, gently at first and then more firmly, until finally she pressed one finger between them to be rewarded by a warm and moist passage. From inside the stricken bird-girl's lips came a whine of protestation that quickly dissolved into an altogether different sound. Oona began to whimper now as the scent of female arousal reached her keen nostrils.

'Not yet, you greedy bitch.' Jane laughed. 'You've had one prize already, so this one is mine. Don't worry though,' she added, seeing the resentful expression in Oona's eyes, 'I'll only be flavouring her for you. After all, I don't have quite all of your advantages for the actual stuffing.'

Rocking back and forth astride the fallen trunk in a steadily increasing rhythm, Kitty was so engrossed in her own needs that she neither saw nor heard the approach of the two men until they were virtually upon her. Gasping and groaning, she slowed herself to a gentle swaying motion and stared at the newcomers through hooded eyes all but hidden from them by her mask.

They were not dressed as hunters, she saw, and instead of specially charged pistols and whips they were carrying muskets. Probably keepers, she told herself, annoyed at them for interrupting her. Perhaps, though, they would be thinking about taking advantage of her helpless situation, and her pulse began to quicken at the thought. But the older man stopped just short of her, and held up a hand as if to try to calm her.

'Just you sit there, me darling,' he said softly. 'Sean and me mean you no harm, we just need a bit of help. Now, can you speak? Ah no, I see you can't. Whatever in the name of all that's holy are these bastards playing at with you girls?'

Kitty made no attempt to reply, and neither did she entirely stop her motion, for the two dildos felt very good as the shifting pressure pushed them in and out, and she was riding very close to the crest of an orgasm. Maybe one of them would...

'Yes, you just let me help you off there,' the one called Sean said, handing his musket to his companion and stepping towards her with an outstretched hand. Kitty mewled in protest as she tried to lean away from him, shaking her head in frustration.

'There now,' the fellow continued, 'there's nothing to be frightened of, it's just me and Paddy, and maybe we can get you out of this accursed devil's kitchen before the day's done. You'd like that now, wouldn't you?'

Moaning and sighing as the man began to lift her clear of the fallen tree, Kitty was not altogether sure she would like that at all.

Isobel could hear the air whistling in and out of her nostrils like the sound of a demented bellows, and she bit hard into her gag as she tried to fight the overwhelming surges of pleasure her captors' attentions were causing her.

Trussed up in such an undignified position, she knew she should have been mortified and horrified. And indeed, for the first few moments as Jane Handiwell (Isobel recognised her voice and mannerisms) went to work on her with the twine, she had been enraged and embarrassed to be treated this way by a girl who was a commoner. However, almost as soon as Jane's fingers began to probe and explore the tightly compressed lips of her exposed sex, Isobel's baser instincts began taking over. Now, as the dog-girl's rough tongue rasped in and out of her pussy, lapping eagerly at a clitoris that had grown hard and bold, she could smell her own arousal and feel how wet she was between her thighs. Had either of them been male, they could have taken her with ease, for her usually tight tunnel was now so well lubricated that no amount of resistance on her part could have prevented an easy entry into her body.

She groaned and screwed her eyes shut as she heard Jane's mocking laughter. Did the common little bitch suspect who she was? The identifying ribbon had come loose before they captured her, so to the Handiwell wench she could easily be just another of the bird-girls, but there was something that suggested to Isobel that Jane knew who she was...

'Wait on, Oona,' she heard Jane command, and immediately the insistent tongue ceased its work. 'Ah yes, the bitch is lovely and wet now.' She stroked Isobel's sex. 'Well done, Oona, you shall have her properly in a few moments, but first I think we should tenderise this lovely rump she's offering us.'

As the first stroke of the whip fell across Isobel's naked buttocks the hapless aristocrat knew she had been right: she was going to be made to pay for the slights and put-downs to which she had subjected the innkeeper's daughter ever since they met. Worse still, she knew, the whip would do more than hurt her, for its fierce caress was doing nothing to quench the fires burning inside her. Although she flinched and whined beneath each stroke, the silently demanding screams of desire rising from deep within her flesh sounded louder inside her head than any cries she could utter through her gagged mouth.

'Titty Kitty?' Paddy echoed. 'What manner of name is that, girl?' He stood holding the shivering bird- girl by the arm, her sodden gag hanging from his free hand.

'It's what they call me, sir,' Kitty mumbled, looking down at his feet, 'because of these.' She tried to indicate her burgeoning breasts with her winged arm, but she could barely bend it.

'They're certainly a pair of beauties,' Sean Kelly observed, but Paddy Riley's warning glance silenced him before he could make any further remarks.

'Well... Kitty,' Paddy continued, 'tell me this, how many of you are here in these woods? I mean, how many girls are running around like this?'

Kitty pursed her lips thoughtfully. 'I'm not sure, sir, five or six, I think. Or maybe seven, I can't remember. There was this funny girl who bet she could do it better, and we had to wait until they got her ready.'

'And how many men are hunting you?'

Kitty sounded even more uncertain. 'Maybe as many as ten,' she said, but Paddy could see this was just a guess. 'And one of them is a woman,' she added, this time sounding more definite. 'She's dressed the same, but she's a woman, and then there's also this dog-woman.' She shuddered. 'She has nasty teeth and horrible eyes,' she whispered, peering up into Paddy's face, 'and they give her these horrible claws, all shiny and sharp! I hope someone catches me before they do. Or have you caught me first?'

Paddy grunted. 'Looks like that's exactly what we've done, Kitty,' he said, 'but then our purpose is a mite different from those others, or my name isn't Riley.'

'Oh,' Kitty said, 'you mean you're not going to...?'

'No,' Paddy said quickly. 'No, we're not going to.' He smiled encouragingly down at her, and to his astonishment saw a definite glint of disappointment in her half-hidden eyes. 'No,' he repeated, 'but we're going to let the next man along here think he's got every chance of doing just that.'

Guy Bressingham listened to the slow tolling of the tower bell as it echoed through the woods, and smiled to himself. The sound meant Isobel had won her bet, but this did not worry him in the least. He had calculated that his chances of capturing her within the specified hour were probably not much better than one in four, and the money involved he had considered written off before the hunt even began. His smile widened into a grin. The money meant nothing to him; he had inherited a medium-sized fortune and had since managed his affairs so well it was now a good-sized fortune. No, the money was as nothing to him, but Isobel... now there was a prize worth having, and have her he would. For the stupid girl had not specified that she was to be released at the end of the hour, only that if she stayed free for that time she would receive the money. Bressingham would happily honour that end of the bargain. The money was already in Grayling's hands ready to be paid over to Isobel when the hunt was over.

When the hunt was over.

Bressingham snickered to himself as he plodded along the trail. The hunt included the after-hunt celebrations and Isobel had volunteered herself for this part of the proceedings, that ended only when the birds had been enjoyed by their captors. He and Grayling had discussed the matter thoroughly; there could be no contesting that, when Bressingham finally caught his bird then he would have the right to her as much as any other hunter would have the right to his own catch.

She would hate it, he knew, but then she would have no means to protest against the decision since the leather gags the girls wore beneath their bird masks prevented any comprehensible speech. Neither would she be able to free herself. The stiffened leather of the tightly laced wings had been well designed; once in place the wearer could not remove them, and neither could she use her hands for anything remotely dextrous.

No, Isobel de Lednay would remain a bird until well into the night, perhaps even until the following morning. Bressingham felt his pulse begin to quicken at the thought. He could almost feel himself sliding into her defenceless pussy, her beautiful backside raised towards him so invitingly by the traditional trussing he would enjoy carrying out first. It had taken all his control to restrain himself when she first appeared in her gaudy outfit, her breasts invitingly exposed between her feathers, her sex lips bulging enticingly from either side of the gusset strap holding the plugging shafts inside her.

'She'll maybe not like the thought,' Grayling had said, 'but by the time she's run around in the woods with those things in her arse and pussy, she'll be hot for something, believe me, and she won't be able to help herself if you stuff her thoroughly!'

Bressingham had been astonished when Grayling suggested the scheme to him earlier that day. He was aware that Isobel and Roderick had known each other for a long time, and that Isobel was sweet on the young landowner's son, so much so that he was able to treat her with the utmost contempt at times and yet she was still not swayed from him. But this deliberate conniving to deliver her helpless into the clutches of another man... would she ever forgive him *this?* But then, he thought, she would never be told it had been Grayling's idea in the first place. And she had played into their hands so easily, rising to the bait so quickly, she could hardly blame anyone but herself for whatever happened to her.

Grayling would play the part, all right. He would shrug his shoulders and sympathise, but then he would insist the rules were the rules, the same for everyone, and he could not break them or make even the smallest exception, not even for her. Perhaps *especially* not for her, for people would then surely accuse him of favouritism.

He would repay Isobel for her rebuffs, for her thinly veiled insults, for her sarcastic quips and her constant parading and flaunting before him, which she knew had such an effect on him. 'I'll parade you all right, bird-slut!' he hissed as he paused at another junction in the path. 'You'll make a pretty enough picture wriggling on the end of my cock on the main table tonight, and you'll remember your stuffing for many a year to come!'

Isobel had long since lost count of the number of small orgasms Jane's whip and her probing finger had triggered within her. Held rigidly by the cunning twine bindings, her head down and her buttocks raised, she gasped against her gag as fiery darts of ecstasy pierced her through and through.

Twice Jane had stood back and let the dog-girl at her, the bitch's long tongue pressing inside her like a small penis, its rough surface working on her throbbing clitoris with devastating effect. Time and again Isobel came, whining and wriggling, panting and moaning until she could no longer tell whether it was tongue, finger or whip her body was responding to so fiercely.

Finally the combined assault ceased, and although Isobel's vision was still hazy, and her other senses were equally befuddled by her ordeal, she was dimly aware that Jane was speaking.

'Now, Oona, you can let the birdie see what the nice doggie has for her. Come around so she can look at you, there's a good dog.'

Isobel felt a sharp kick in her side and tried to look back at Jane, but the cording prevented her from turning her head very far, and the eye-slits deprived her of any periphery vision.

'Wake up, slut-bird!' Jane commanded. 'Here, look up and see what the nice doggie has for you!'

Blearily, Isobel peered out of her mask aware that a dark shape had moved around before her. She blinked, trying to focus on Oona, and then blinked again, this time in sheer disbelief. *The dog-girl has a cock!* her brain screamed even as all her mouth could manage was a whimper of horror. Oona, who had earlier been all too obviously female, was now all too obviously male, at least from the groin down. Isobel kept blinking, trying to see whether the organ now jutting so threateningly up before the dog-girl's navel was a trick, an artificial phallus strapped to her waist... but no, there was little doubt that it was real. It emerged from between the lips where normally a particularly responsive clitoris might appear, the dark-blue veins decorating it straining against the stretched and gleaming flesh.

'My doggie is going to fuck you now, birdie.' Jane laughed. 'Her cock is going to skewer you good, too. I've seen her in action before and she'll outlast any man you care to name, won't you Oona, my pet?'

The dog-girl growled on cue, but this time Isobel could have sworn the growl turned into a gratified chuckle.

Crawley's remaining original assistant, Silas Grout, had taken charge of the proceedings on the green. There was no sign of his master as the newly recruited men dragged Harriet from the church, her eyes blinking in the harsh sunlight after her long stint in a gloomy crypt. They led her over to a position opposite the graveyard, where the curious execution platform had been set up beneath the tallest oak. However, it was still a few hours until sunset, the appointed hour for the hanging, and first there was the matter of Wickstanner's funeral.

Grout - or perhaps the instruction had come from Crawley himself - had taken a certain amount of care to ensure that not only would Harriet have a clear view of the burial, but also that the villagers would have a clear view of her and her shame. A heavy post had been driven into the ground before which stood a trestle bench some three feet high. Onto this bench two men hoisted Harriet, and then Grout himself, standing on one end, took up a long staff which he passed through the crook formed in her elbow by the cuff holding her left wrist to the waist-belt. Pressing her back against the upright, he thrust the pole in further so it passed behind the post, and then grabbing her other elbow cruelly, he forced the wooden bar through the crook on that side. Now she was not only held against the post but her shoulders were bent back painfully and her naked breasts were thrust forward in an obscene parody of temptation. Harriet grunted, trying to shift her position to ease the strain, but it was impossible.

'There now, you can show your nice titties off to all the world one last time,'

Grout said quietly, so only she could hear him. He moved in front of her, the trestle so narrow he was forced to press up against her, and Harriet felt his hand grope between her thighs as he did so. To her utter chagrin, she realised her recent ordeal had left her sex wet and open, and she immediately tried to pull her thighs together. Grout, however, was having none of it.

'Must let the good people see there's no devil's spawn hiding in there,' he hissed, jumping down onto the grass. He signalled to one of the men, who stepped forward holding two coils of rope. Within a matter of seconds they had snared each of her ankles and dragged her legs wide apart, tying the ropes to either end of the trestle.

Tears stung Harriet's eyes, for she knew her plight would surely attract the attention of the people as they began gathering for the funeral. The men-folk might try to affect an attitude of piety for the benefit of their female relatives, but few would be able to resist staring at her nudity.

Silas Grout was not quite finished, however. One of the new assistants had been despatched across the short span of grass separating Harriet's perch from the wagon, and he returned carrying a piece of board on which had been painted, in large red letters, DEVIL WHORE AND WITCH. Beneath this legend, in smaller print, had been added, *Sentenced this day, by order of the Holy Church*. A length of cord had been knotted through two small holes so the sign could be hung about her neck, and Grout held it up for her to read before doing so. He also, she realised, had made sure the board hung beneath her breasts and above her crotch, thus not affording her any modesty nor obstructing the view for the lascivious eyes that would soon be feasting on her.

She closed her eyes and tried to shut out the horror of it all. The board bore no date and she shuddered as she realised it had probably been painted without one so it could be used over and over again. She wondered how many other terrified and mortally ashamed females had stood as she did now with this piece of wood hanging from their necks counting the minutes to their death.

'There now,' Grout said, jumping down onto the grass for the last time and stepping back to look up at her. 'That should make sure anyone else in this place thinks twice before they start meddling with the dark arts.' He turned to the five men who had gathered in a half circle before Harriet. 'You lot had better make sure no one gets near her. Can't be too careful when it comes to witching, so make sure you're all wearing the crosses Master Crawley gave you. The whore's powers should be just about scourged from her, I reckon, but it's better to be safe than sorry, I always says.' He turned to Thaddeus Gilbert. 'You're in charge till I get back. Anything happens while I'm gone and it won't just be getting paid you have to worry about. I'm going to wet my whistle for an hour, but I should be back before they start lowering the vicar. Once that's over you bring the girl over to the tree, and I'll need a couple of you to help get her up onto that bit that sticks out under the noose there.'

Harriet opened her eyes, and for the first time saw that there was indeed a rope hanging from one of the thick branches of the oak with a noose already tied and waiting. There also seemed to be another loop in it halfway up its length, but she was too far away to make out what it was exactly, or to understand its purpose.

The hunt was approaching the end of its second hour, Guy Bressingham calculated, looking up at the position of the sun in the sky. Two hours nearly gone and he had seen not one sign of life, not even one of the other bird-girls.

He paused alongside a fallen tree trunk that had been stripped bare of its branches and leaves quite recently, to judge from the freshness of the axe marks, and lowered himself onto it, relieved to take the weight off his feet, which were beginning to ache. He was not, he was forced to admit, used to such strenuous exercise; he rarely walked much further than the door of his carriage these days. He sighed, and bent to loosen his right boot.

Isobel de Lednay could wait awhile yet, he decided. Her marker ribbon guaranteed that none of the other hunters would attempt to take her. His toes were throbbing, and a few minutes of freedom from the restricting boots would be more than welcome. There was also the small brandy flask in his belt pouch. A bracing reviver was the order of the day.

He was about to kick off his first boot when the sound of rustling leaves made him look up. There, to his amazement, stood one of the other bird-girls. No, she wasn't standing; she was walking - walking straight towards him without fear.

'Well!' he exclaimed, sitting up, 'what do we have here? A tired birdie maybe, or just tired of running around? I can sympathise with that, to be sure.' He stood up slowly, not wanting to startle the girl, who continued to approach him slowly. 'Decided to get it over with? Well, I can't say I blame you. It's inevitable anyway, and I'm sure you know that.' His eyes narrowed as he studied her. 'Ah yes,' he continued, 'I remember you, the girl with the big titties, and what a fine pair they are too.' She stood before him, staring mutely up at him through the eye-slits of her colourful mask. 'Well, there's no rule says I can't take two of you, I suppose,' he said, feeling the warmth from her body now, and the manner in which her large breasts were rising and falling was all too appealing. It was Isobel he really wanted, but then Isobel was his anyway. Meanwhile, he had this creature for the taking, and her attitude seemed to indicate she wanted him as much as he now wanted her. 'Somehow,' he said, placing a hand on each of her shoulders, 'I don't think I'm going to have to waste any time with all that trussing up nonsense, eh?'

Isobel groaned as the head of Oona's male organ pressed against her labia and pushed it apart as easily as a hot knife passing through butter. Steel claws grasped at either side of her breasts, compressed and pushed outwards between her ribs and her thighs, but to her surprise, the dog-girl did not set about ravishing her with the sort of ferocity her demeanour led one to expect. Instead, she let Isobel feel the end of her throbbing shaft slowly settling within her, allowing her to anticipate the great length that would soon be thrusting in and out of her.

'Good dog, Oona,' Jane said from somewhere behind them. 'Yes, just let her settle nicely, there's a good girl. My, but what artist wouldn't give his left arm for the chance to paint this picture?'

Isobel was certain now that the innkeeper's daughter knew exactly who she was and was deliberately drawing out her humiliation. But did she also know just how her victim's body was reacting to its ordeal? She closed her eyes and tried to slow her breathing, tried to ignore both the dog-girl's presence at one entrance to her body and the muscle-stretching leather dildo still filling her other orifice. She knew she should at least attempt to expel it now that the crotch-strap no longer held it in place, but why bother? There was nothing at all she could do to prevent what was happening to her, nor what was still to come. Jane Handiwell was going to enjoy every moment of this, so why, Isobel reasoned grimly, shouldn't she do so herself?

As the long shaft finally began to glide deeper into her pussy, Isobel opened her eyes again, and with a groaning cry of exaltation, pushed herself backwards with all her strength the inch or so her bondage permitted. A moment later, as Oona withdrew halfway, and then slammed deep into her hot cleft a second time, Isobel was blinded by the first of what she knew was likely to be a very long sequence of climaxes.

Silas Grout explained whilst miming the action of snapping a twig between his two hands. He had finished his second flagon of ale now and was waiting as the serving girl refilled it from one of the barrels behind the counter, his back to her as he faced his audience. There were about a dozen men in the taproom, and his monologue had caught the attention of them all.

'We loop the rope up and tie it about with a length of thin thread which breaks when the witch drops, and lets her go on down till just before her feet reach the ground. Then the rope snaps tight. Dead in an instant, just like that!' He snapped his fingers to emphasise his point. 'Of course,' he continued, sniffing and wiping his sleeve across his mouth and nose, 'I reckon it'd be better to let them have their little dance before they choke, but Master Crawley is a kind Christian soul and hates to see unnecessary suffering.'

'And what do you call taking the lash to a poor defenceless girl and stripping her of all her clothes and dignity?' Thomas Handiwell strode into the room through the door leading to his private quarters, pushed his way past the knot of drinkers, and stood squarely before Grout. 'Is that the work of a man who hates to see unnecessary suffering?' he demanded.

Grout half turned, took up the flagon the girl had placed at his elbow, and shrugged. 'That's *necessary* suffering, that is. When Satan possesses a witch, then there's only one way to drive his evilness out of her, and that's with the lash. Then it's down to making sure the bastard has nowhere to lurk and try to claim her back when we've done. Tricky swine, the Devil, but then he's been that way since he tempted Eve.'

'Nonsense!' Thomas bellowed. 'I know for a fact that the lord bishops decreed there were no such things as witches. This is all balderdash, and whatever work it is that you and your master are about, it's not that of the good Lord!'

'No such thing as witches?' Grout lifted one eyebrow and looked slowly from left to right. The watching faces were all expectant now, anticipating a clash between the executioner's assistant and the innkeeper. 'No such thing as witches?' he repeated. 'Well, if that's so, what else could possibly have possessed your good vicar and ripped his head clean off his shoulders? I call that witchcraft or the devil's work by any other name.'

There was a low murmur of assent.

'The fool Wickstanner took his own life,' Thomas said evenly. 'He was probably addled with drink and guilt at being responsible for what's happened to that poor wench out there. The way I heard it, he jumped off a ladder with a rope about his fool neck and it was that tore his head off, not some supernatural monster as you'd like these poor fools to believe.'

'Here,' said an indignant voice at the rear of the spectators, 'I don't like being called no fool.'

'Then don't act like one, Josh Avery,' Thomas snapped, recognising the speaker without needing to turn his head. 'I had you marked as a man with some sense, and now I find you in here with this motley bunch, hanging on the every word of a man who's probably got more innocent blood on his hands than I've had hot stews.'

'So, innkeeper,' Grout sneered, 'you take it upon yourself to decide who is innocent and who is not, do you? Master Crawley has all the proper warrants, and the authority of this and many other parishes to carry out God's work. So have a care, or else people here might think you're trying to blacken us just to save that witch, and then they might wonder just why a so-called honest innkeeper should be so worried about her. We already know she has the old woman and the miller's boy in league with her, and that they murdered a good and true servant of the Church, for which crime they'll answer in due course, I can assure you. Maybe you want to see your name added to that warrant as well?'

There was a mixture of muffled laughter and mutterings indicating possible agreement, but Thomas was unmoved even though he knew there was little point in trying to interfere. If Brotherwood sent troops up from the coast, then maybe the girl's life could be saved, for he was certain Crawley and his cohorts were acting illegally. But meantime, these ignorant fools would not dare to back him against a man they believed was acting for the Church.

On the other hand, there was something he *could* do, no matter how little the naked girl standing waiting to die would benefit from it. He reached out, and before Grout could react seized the flagon of ale from his hand and dashed it to the floor. 'Well,' he snarled, 'if you're so worried about my integrity, then I'm sure you wouldn't want to risk drinking in my establishment.' He kicked the flagon aside and it clattered against the base of the counter. 'So, you'd oblige me, master so-called hangman, if you'd take your custom elsewhere, for it's not welcome under this roof and neither are you!

'And as for my name on any warrant,' Thomas continued, his voice icy, 'I don't think I'm the one who needs to worry about that.'

'You know what's to be done.' It was a statement rather than a question. Adam Portfield knew his younger cousin, Daniel, had been involved in two of these special hunting events since his arrival at Grayling Hall at the beginning of the summer, and that his brother's eldest son was also a bright lad and a quick learner. 'Just take your time and use your eyes. Some of them don't bother staying around to wait for their catch to be collected, but they're at least supposed to get them to the side of the nearest path and tie one of the yellow markers somewhere easy to spot at the closet fork back this way. They should have put their own markers about the girls' necks, so go careful you don't pull any off by mistake.'

'What if they don't have any markers?' Daniel grinned back at his cousin, the inference obvious in his expression.

Adam shrugged. 'If they don't have a marker, then that's not your fault and there's not much you can do about it until we gets all the birds back here. Then they can sort it out amongst themselves, but there's not usually any problem.'

'What if I find any still on the loose?' Daniel asked. 'Do I catch 'em and put 'em in the wagon with the others?' He nodded to the small wooden vehicle that stood, its patient horse grazing contentedly, by the side of the main path from the barn.

'Best not,' Adam said, 'at least not until after the second bell, and then don't waste any time getting back here with what you have. Any that's still out there will come back soon enough after they've had a night out there with nothing to eat or drink. There's often one who thinks she's a bit smarter'n the others, but after the first time they try to get themselves picked up before dark.'

'I thought most of this clutch were new girls,' Daniel observed.

Adam nodded. 'Aye, that's true enough,' he agreed. "Twas a mistake selling as many of the experienced ones as we did last month, but then his nibs insisted, and he didn't want to let down that French crowd. Something to do with their king's birthday, apparently, but it's none of my business.'

'There's some promising ones from the past few days' intake,' Daniel said.

Adam smiled, because the lad was already sounding like an expert. Indeed, he had shown himself to be well suited to the job here. Tall and well-muscled, even though the wiriness of youth was still awkwardly apparent in his movements, he could have had his pick of the women in any village, and Adam had noticed how the slaves here tended to watch him more closely than they did any of the other overseers. 'Well, we're going to have our work cut out, and no mistake,' he replied. 'I'm going to need to go up to London again soon and see if we can't find ourselves a few new suppliers' names. Business is looking up, especially with so many white slaves wanted for the Indies. It's going to be busy around here over the next few months.'

'Fine by me,' Daniel declared, turning towards the wagon. 'The more we are, the merrier, as they say.'

'Aye, and don't you get back here too late by getting too merry with those girls, either,' Adam warned him. 'A quick tupping or two is fine, but you mind you don't go making too much of a meal of it, and don't let any of the hunters see you getting in on their game. You and George Hawkin are just supposed to be the deliverymen.'

'Yes, cousin,' Daniel said soberly, but both of them knew he would sample every single girl he found, as indeed would the older George Hawkin, who had been driving wagons for the estate and taking care of such unusual cargo ever since the inception of the Grayling operation. 'And I leave everything to the west of the old drive path to George.' He raised a hand in salute and strode away across the grass, whistling tunelessly.

'Right,' Adam called after him, 'and make sure you give each girl a drink when you find her. You can bet your life the buggers don't bother lubricating that end of 'em when they're caught, so they're probably gasping for water by the time you find 'em. Even more than you're gasping for the other thing right now,' he added under his breath.

'He's still breathing, Paddy,' Sean Kelly said, rolling the unconscious black-garbed and masked figure over onto his back and pressing his fingers against the side of his neck.

'Well, I only gave him a small tap on the side of the head,' Paddy explained. 'No point in killing a man unnecessarily, especially not when his back's turned and his cock's taking all his attention. Somehow, that's not quite sporting, is it?'

Kitty, who had been the sole focus of the unfortunate hunter when Paddy pounced on him from the bushes, groaned as she sat up. The gag had been replaced in her mouth for the sake of authenticity, and now she could only stare silently at the scene before her.

'Get that stuff off him,' Paddy ordered, 'and then find something to tie him up with, in case he comes around. Here,' he said, offering Kitty a hand, 'let's have you up and get that thing out of your mouth again. Maybe it'd be put to better use on him,' he added. 'Wouldn't do to have him hollering for help before we're finished.' He stared down at the prone figure as Kelly set to work loosening his clothing. 'I reckon he's near enough my size,' he observed, 'so now all we need to do is find another one about the same stamp as you, me lad.'

Her limbs grown mercifully numb, Harriet hung limply in her bondage, her eyes closed against the lowering sun and against the prying gazes of the village men beginning to venture closer to her scaffold. Crawley's recruits would keep them back and prevent them from actually touching her, she knew, but they would do nothing to stop them getting their fill of her nakedness, and they themselves could not resist the occasional taunt at her expense.

The afternoon was growing late and shadows were beginning to stretch across the grass... two hours until sunset, perhaps a little more. She tried not to think of her father and how he would feel when news of her death reached him. The shock might well finish him off, and perhaps that was for the best. To live on as he was without her there to care for him, and to suffer the knowledge of how shameful her end had been, that was too horrible to contemplate. The fact that she had been done to death mistakenly, in the place of another, would do nothing to ease his shame, and neither would it bring her back to him.

She half opened one eye and peered down at the little group of spectators. They were all faces she knew well enough, and it was no surprise to see them gawking up at her. There were even women amongst them now, two stone-faced old biddies who worked at the mill, and a younger woman who sometimes worked for Thomas Handiwell cleaning bedrooms and sweeping floors at the *Black Drum*.

Poor Thomas, she thought. His shame would be even worse than her father's if he ever discovered the truth about his beloved Jane. But then a father's love is blind, and Jane was as devious and deceitful as her father was straightforward and honest. Would he ever know of her murderous treachery? Despite everything, Harriet found herself praying he never would.

Jane leaned back against the tree as she watched Oona relentlessly penetrating the hapless Isobel with her monstrous erection. She had loosened the belt of her breeches and unhooked the front far enough to enable her to insert one hand down into her crotch, and she was working her fingers into her wet cleft in time with the dog-girl's thrusts.

'Common taproom whore, am I?' Jane whispered to herself, repeating one of the insults she knew the young noblewoman had used when describing her to one of the guests at the hall that summer. She longed to pull Oona off Isobel, throw the aristocratic bitch onto her back and straddle her arrogant face. She wanted to force her to use her mouth to finish off what her own fingers had started, but that would mean giving her victim back the use of her tongue, which would make it difficult to explain why she had not released the silly creature for Bressingham to find.

'No, my lady,' Jane hissed beneath her breath, 'maybe you're more suited to the dog fucking you after all.' Somewhere in the distance a shot rang out, but Jane barely registered it. Vaguely, she wondered if the marksman had found his target, and considered the possibility of allowing Isobel to escape long enough to feel the burning sting of a shot in her buttocks. But for the moment there would be no dragging Oona from her victim until she had sated her animal lust. After that, she really ought to start back towards the house with her, for ferocious as the bizarre creature already seemed, without the regular dosages of the herbal extracts Roderick Grayling bought from his contact in London, she would quickly grow even wilder still. Oona was capable of turning on her handlers when even the threat of the whip did nothing except heighten her

90

murderous rage. Besides, news from the village was that Jacob Crawley intended to hang the girl he still thought of as Matilda Pennywise at sunset, and Jane was determined to be there to watch. Of course, there was a chance the so-called witchfinder might discover his mistake before that, but it was not likely, not now that three of his latest converts had been quietly paid to make sure the mask and bridle were not removed before the sentence was carried out.

On the ground, Isobel was moaning and whining. She sounded as much like a dog as the hermaphroditic human canine Oona. Jane sniggered, and then groaned herself as a small orgasmic shock surged through her, forcing her to grab the tree trunk with her free hand as her knees buckled. 'Ah, yes,' she gasped, 'no doubting who the real bitch is now, my not-so-proud little lady, even though you *do* look more bird than dog at the moment.'

'The innkeeper fellow could be trouble, Master Crawley,' Silas Grout muttered.

Crawley frowned and peered through the small window beside of the main church door. Outside, a few people were already gathered by the graveyard wall, but their attention was more on the spectacle provided by Harriet than on the forthcoming funeral of their beloved clergyman. 'Times have changed, Silas,' he said, 'and not for the better. Only a few years back, no man would have dared speak up against the righteousness of our work, and yet now even the bishops have their liberals among them.' He turned back to stare down the gloomy length of the church, in particular at the dark stain that spread across several of the flagstones. 'Wickstanner was a fool, but no worse than many of his fellows nowadays. They'll like as not send another in his place that's even more stupid. I should have realised what his game was a lot sooner than I did.'

'Revenge is a terrible driving force, master,' Grout said. 'But now we're involved far too deep to pull back, surely?'

'I think so,' Crawley said. 'Besides, the Pennywise wench is evil, and no argument about that, not in my book. She'll drop as she should, and then we'll away from here during the night.'

'What about the old witch and her money?' Grout prompted.

Crawley chuckled, an awful grating sound. 'There's still time for that. I think she'll show up to try and save her damned granddaughter, but the villagers will grab her and keep her out of our way. They may even hang her and the miller's boy for us.'

'You think they really did kill?'

'Of course!' Crawley snapped. 'Who else could it have been? The lad was chained up and now he's seen with the crone, so one or the other of them must have done it. I'd like to see the pair of them dangle for that, but it may be more prudent for us to move on sooner - just as soon as we have her money, of course.'

'And if she doesn't come to us?'

'Ah, but she will, Silas, my faithful old friend,' Crawley assured him with an air of absolute certainty. 'She'll come all right, and she'll do it while the whole village is gathered for this funeral, thinking to use them as protection against us and to barter for the girl's worthless life in full public view. She won't be expecting them to turn against her, and when that happens it'll be too late, especially if we let those ignorant peasants think she's offering to buy the girl back with money they've taken from their poor dead victim!'

'Did you hear that?' Sean Kelly's head jerked up as the sound of the shot echoed through the treetops, sending several birds skywards flapping their wings and squawking in protest at being so rudely disturbed. Ahead of them on the trail, Kitty paused also paused to look up, and then kept walking.

Paddy Riley grimaced. 'Of course I bloody heard it!' he snapped. 'Do you think I'm deaf?' He stood stock still, tilting his head slightly to one side. 'Pistol, I think. Those bastards yesterday were using muskets.'

'The girl said something about them using pistols for this hunt,' Sean reminded him.

Paddy grunted, his lips twisting into a grim smile beneath the black mask he now wore, the mask that, together with the black breeches and jerkin, they had stripped from the captured hunter. 'She said a whole lot of things and barely one of them made much sense.'

'You think they kill the poor things?'

'I shouldn't think so,' Paddy retorted gruffly. 'They wouldn't go to all that trouble just for that. No, the lass said something about the shots stinging and bruising. Probably using some kind of wadded slug. Painful at short range, but it wouldn't kill.'

'This is one mad and heathen place,' Sean muttered. 'The sooner we get this done and back to real fighting, the better I'll like it.'

'Amen to that,' Paddy agreed, and suddenly stiffening reached out to grab Sean's upper arm.

The younger trooper responded immediately; a second later both men were crouching between two clumps of bushes to one side of the path.

'Up ahead there, I think,' Paddy whispered. 'I saw a figure, and then he was gone off to the side there on the left.'

'You think he saw us, too?' Sean whispered.

Paddy shrugged. 'If he did, we're probably too far off for him to think we're anything but more of their own heathen kind. In this little lot he'd take me for one of them, and you could be one of their keepers. Besides, he'll be more interested in yon poor wench and being the first to grab her to pay us much heed, and by the time he does it'll be too late.'

'What I can't understand,' Sean said quietly, sounding puzzled, 'is why the girl doesn't really seem all that scared. If I didn't know better, I'd say she was actually a bit annoyed we came upon her like we did. Anyone'd think she didn't want to be rescued from all this, and I know that can't be true.'

Silas Grout stood back beneath the shadow of a large oak by the graveyard wall and watched the proceedings with an air of detached amusement. The funeral cortege had continued growing even as the coffin was being borne from the church, but this was no surprise to Silas. No matter how ineffectual or unpopular Wickstanner might have been, he had still been God's representative in the parish, and in the eyes of his parishioners it was their duty to see him off on his final journey.

The sun was low in the sky now and Silas had counted more than two hundred people already by the time the coffin bearers reached the side of the newly dug grave, and more were still hurrying across the green even at this late stage. Crawley, who had followed the coffin, stood at the other side of the grave, his head bowed as he waited for the crowd to settle.

'Hey, mister!' The urgent voice was barely more than a whisper but its sudden intrusion into his reverie made Grout jump. He spun around, his hand already reaching for his pistol in an instinctive gesture, and found himself confronted with a fresh-faced youngster staring up at him from over the top of the stone wall.

Grout wagged an admonishing finger at him. 'Bugger off, you little bastard,' he hissed. 'Go on, be off with you, before I stick my boot where the sun don't shine.'

The lad seemed totally unimpressed by this threat. 'You Crawley's man, mister?' he demanded in a tone that indicated he already knew the answer.

Grout's eyes narrowed. 'What's it to you, you grubby little whippersnapper?'

'Got something for you, that's what,' the lad replied smugly. 'I was told to give it to you or to Crawley, and seeing as how he's looking a bit busy just now, I thought I'd best give it to you.'

'Oh?' Grout leaned on the wall and peered over it.

The youth was crouched down on the grass on the other side, and he held up a small leather purse together with a rolled piece of parchment. 'There's gold in the bag,' he said, 'and the message is writ down on the other. If you can read, then read it, if not, give it to Crawley when they've done burying the priest, that's what they told me to say.' He grinned wickedly.

'And who might *they* be?' Grout demanded, annoyed by the boy's confidence and by the fact that he seemed to think he could give orders to his elders and betters.

'Tells you that in the letter,' the boy snapped as Grout took purse and parchment from him. And then he was up and running before Grout could even think about trying to grab him. 'Make sure Crawley gets that as soon as they've done the burying,' the boy called back, pausing once he was safely out of reach. 'And tell him that if he hangs the girl, then he won't see another penny and his soul will be damned for evermore!'

It was only a dream, Sarah knew, but unlike every other dream she could recall, even the most terrible of nightmares, knowing this did not give her the power to wake herself up.

She stood in a small glade, the bright sun shafting down through gaps in the leaves above, wild flowers glowing with unnatural colours around the base of the trees encircling the small clearing. She was naked, free of even the leather harness that had been used to enslave her, but she seemed to be captive to a different form of bondage now...

Peering down through the deep valley between her breasts, she saw that her feet had somehow changed, that they were no longer her feet at all for they were not even human. In place of toes she now stood perched upon two dainty hooves, and when she held up her arms, she saw her hands had become catlike paws with wickedly curving claws in place of nails. A short, downy fur ran up the backs of her arms almost to her elbows, giving her skin a mottled, almost leopard-like, effect.

He would come for her soon, she knew, and trying to run away was hopeless. Wherever she ran, he would follow her and find her for he knew her, and he knew these magical woods and every hiding place she might seek. She peered down again and this time noticed that her nose seemed to be longer and also to have grown wider, forming a fur-covered snout. The revelation neither surprised nor upset her, for she knew her new form was what he desired for her so she could be free of everything that once encumbered her.

She looked up again and was not surprised to see him standing at the edge of the woods just a few paces from her. He was smiling and staring at her with that peculiar expression that meant he knew she was his to command. 'Come, Sarah,' he said, speaking softly and extending a hand to her. She noticed that he too was naked and hoofed, and his manhood was standing erect and proud as if bidding her to him. Slowly, revelling in her newfound grace, she moved towards him and dropped to her knees at his feet unbidden, reaching eagerly with her open mouth to take the head of his massive shaft between her lips.

'My sweet little fawn girl,' he said, and she felt his hands stroking the fur covering her skull.

Greedily, Sarah sucked, raising her head and bending her neck forward until she had taken the entire impossible length of his erect penis into her mouth and down into her throat. And then, very slowly, she drew back again, letting the glistening erection emerge from between her lips until once again only the head remained held in her slippery grip. And finally, releasing him completely, she stood up. She turned, and placing her pawed hands upon her hips, bent at the waist until her head almost touched the ground while moving her hoofed feet further apart to present herself to him for mating. 'Master,' she breathed, but the sound came out like a plaintive bleating. She turned her head, begging him with her eyes as her tongue apparently could not, but he knew what she desired and there was no need for words. She felt him pressing into her, parting her swollen nether lips and pushing further and further until at last he filled her up completely.

'Sweet fawn,' he said, 'I knew you would understand, and now you are mine.' He withdrew from her slightly, paused, and then slid fully into her again.

Sarah felt her stomach and heart lurch, and the fires that had been merely embers until now began to fan up into flames she knew would consume her very soul and make her one with him forever.

Kitty lay back against the base of the tree, breathless and trembling, both from the sudden ferocity of Paddy's assault and from the passions her latest captor had succeeded in arousing in her before the butt of Paddy's musket clubbed him senseless. Although the two men had dragged the hunter off her, she could still feel his throbbing cock inside her and she wanted to shout out that it wasn't fair to leave her like this. However, as she watched them stripping the black garb from the unconscious man, all she could do was chew on her leather gag in silent frustration.

'He's near enough your size, Sean,' Paddy was saying. 'Maybe a bit longer in the leg, but you can tuck the breeches inside the boots and no one will notice anything.'

'Except I'm going to feel like a complete fool in that mask thing,' Sean retorted. 'I just hope this is all going to be worth it. It's all very well disguising ourselves, but there's a hell of a lot of woods out here, and we're looking for one poor lass that's probably as hard to spot for herself as this one here.'

'Well, I think I'd have to agree with you there, Sean Kelly,' Paddy said calmly, 'which is why we're not even going to try looking. Besides, from what the little bird tells us, there's no certainty where she might be, either out here, in the house, or wherever. But, if you were listening, as I was, then you'd realise that come nightfall most everyone's going to be back at the house, or in the barn she told us about. After all this running around out here, I daresay there'll be a bit of ale and wine flowing, and that should give us the chance to poke around a bit.'

'And what if we still don't find her?'

'Well,' Paddy sat back on his haunches and peered out through the eye-slits in the mask he had taken from their first victim, 'if we don't, then we don't, and there won't be too much we can do about it. But,' he added, 'I think we might already be halfway to what we came for. The girl we left back there with the lad?'

Sean looked up at him and shrugged. 'What about her? She was rambling, completely out of her head.'

'Maybe so,' Paddy agreed, 'but maybe you weren't trying to listen as hard as I was. She was going on about a coach and highwaymen, or women dressed as highwaymen, I think.'

'Ah,' a light dawned in Sean's eyes. 'You think she might be the cousin?'

Paddy nodded. 'I reckon she might be. Of course, she could be some other poor wench they've seized and brought here, but she'll do, either way. It's one thing for this Grayling to be doing all this with legally bought slaves and bondswomen, but quite another to have free women held and treated like this. If we get our wench back to the inn, and give her time to regain her senses, maybe her testimony will be all Master Handiwell and the captain needs to get a warrant from a magistrate and send in the militia in proper numbers. Of course,' he said again, grinning wryly, 'they might be sending more of our lads up from Portsmouth even as we sit here, so perhaps it'll be us that gets to come back and sort the twisted bastards out properly this time.'

'The old woman writes a surprisingly neat script, master,' Silas Grout observed. After the funeral he had discreetly called the witchfinder back into the church and passed him the note the boy had given him by the churchyard wall.

Jacob Crawley furrowed his brow. 'More likely the miller's lad,' he retorted. 'From what I hear tell, the lad knows his letters well. But 'tis not the style that we need concern ourselves with Silas, but rather the content. You've read this through, I take it?'

Grout nodded. 'Aye, master,' he confirmed. "Twas not sealed, and the lad said I was to read it.'

'Then you'll see we have a problem, or rather a choice. It says here that the gold we have so far is but a small portion of what the old woman will give us in return for her bitch of a granddaughter.'

'A sizeable sum, from what they write there,' Grout agreed.

'Aye,' Crawley mused, 'more than I expected to see offered.'

'Maybe there's more still?'

'As like as not there is,' Crawley said, 'but to waste time even thinking about that would be foolish. No,' he tapped the parchment with his knuckles, 'this is well worth our time as it is, and we'll not risk losing that for sheer greed. I am not a greedy man, Silas, am I?' He stared at Grout, who dutifully shook his head.

'No, Master Crawley, you ain't a greedy man. So, you'll give them the girl?'

'Yes, but they'll not enjoy her company, nor she her freedom, for long. You see, I fear I may have been a little careless in her hearing.'

'Ah...' Grout looked sympathetic. 'We can't risk leaving a wagging tongue in our wake.'

'Indeed not, though it'll be a while before that particular tongue wags again, in any case. Now, let's think this out. You'll have to go to the inn, of course, and say we're agreeable to the terms of the bargain.'

'And what will you tell the village people?' Grout asked. 'They're out there now gawking at the wench and waiting to see me drop her.'

'I'll tell them,' Crawley decided, straightening his shoulders, 'that I have been praying in here for her soul and that my prayers have been answered by her wishing to salve the last of her guilt before she goes to meet her creator.'

'Her guilt as a witch?'

'Her guilt as a murderess,' Crawley said. 'You go out and have her fetched back in here. Tell everyone that I wish for her to be given one last chance to pray before the altar with me, and afterwards we shall say she confessed to the murders of several travellers and agreed to take us to where she buried the bodies. We'll tell them the hanging is postponed until dawn. They'll not mind that too much, even if it means they need to be out of their flea-ridden beds earlier than usual to see it. Our fine new friends will make sure none of the villagers follow us so we can take her out to the agreed meeting place unobserved. Then all we need do afterwards is swear it was an intended trick on her part, and that the old woman and the miller's son tried to surprise us and take her. Of course, after a brave but brief skirmish, we managed to kill them, and then brought the girl back here to be executed in the proper manner.'

'What if the old woman and the lad are indeed armed?' Grout sounded worried.

Crawley smiled at him. 'Oh, I anticipate they will be,' he said, 'but they'll not be able to shoot at us for fear of hitting the girl, and by the time we come up to them and produce our pistols from beneath our capes, it'll be too late. Of course, we'll need to discharge their weapons and perhaps put a ball hole through your sleeve to show how close you came to paying the price of their treachery. That innkeeper and the pretty soldier boy captain are sure to ask questions, so we'll have their answers ready for them.'

She stood before him now, legs astride, head held high, as she reached down to pry apart the lips of her desire. He stood watching quietly, a gentle smile playing across his usually cruel lips, one hand holding his erect passion, the other stroking his chin as if he were lost in thought.

'Master, do I please you?' she asked quietly. Between her fingers she could feel the engorged stiffness of her clitoris jutting defiantly.

He nodded. 'Yes, slave fawn, you do please me,' he said. 'But first I must cleanse your soul and purge all the ill spirits from you. Fetch the implements to me.'

She released her grip on her moist lips, and then turned gracefully and padded across the thickly carpeted floor to the gold-covered table. Her breathing was shallow but also slow and rhythmic as she picked up the things he would need.

Back before him once more, she sank slowly to her knees and placed her hands dutifully behind her back, lowering her shaven head while he moved behind her to secure the golden cuffs around her wrists. The golden collar followed, and the dull clicks as he secured each of the items in turn were like a clock marking the passage of time into her new self.

'You are mine, fawn slave,' he whispered, bending close to her ear.

She nodded almost imperceptibly. 'Yes, master,' she answered in the same reverent tone, 'yes, I am yours, and you should make me deserving of your ownership.'

He picked up the golden-handled whip and paid out the nine long tails hanging from it. Then he bent again and offered the end of the handle to her lips. She parted them, sucking it into her mouth, and then drawing back from it to place a gentle kiss upon it. 'Thank you, master, for the punishment I am about to receive,' she said, raising her eyes to his.

He smiled, nodded, and then moved around behind her.

'I love you, master!' she cried, and the first crack of the whip's fiery tongues across her back sent shivers of delight throughout her entire being. Between her legs the hunger had begun again, and she screamed because she could not move her hands to it. Her master would not want her to, she knew, for only he was permitted to satisfy and fuel it.

The whip fell again, this time the thongs curling around in front of her and wrapping themselves around her hanging breasts, drawing lines of red across her pale flesh and plucking at her bulging nipples. She screamed again, wanting to touch them, to knead them, to offer her full globes the better for him to punish them.

'Patience, my fawn,' he said, as if understanding her desire. 'Patience and contrition and you shall be fulfilled.' He reached down and pinched each of her swollen teats in turn, and then he stood back and the braids whistled through the air once more. Three more times the whip lashed out and she was singing now, calling her surrender to him in words she did not know she understood. And then it was the time and she rose unbidden, turning to where he now sat upon a golden stool, hands at his sides, his member jutting up from his lap. She smiled and shook her head to flick away tears of joy as she approached him. Straddling his knees, she opened herself to him, lowering herself down onto his full length in one impaling thrust.

'Master!' she cried, and his teeth bared as fangs descending into the soft flesh of her neck. He took from her as he gave to her, and she gave herself completely and unreservedly to him...

The wagon, although smaller than the one Sam Hawkin used to bring the slave girls from London to the Hall, was still barely able to pass along the narrow tracks that ran through the woods of the Grayling estate. Daniel Portfield had to concentrate to prevent the wheels from straying off into the softer ground at the edges. The lone horse knew his territory, however, and between them they were able to affect a comfortable progress.

Daniel chewed reflectively on a thick stem of wild grass as he drove. He had hoped not to be chosen as one of the collectors today, for the job would take until it was all but dark and the opportunity to avail himself of any of the captured bird-girls did little to compensate for the boredom in between. After all, he reasoned, back at the barns there were scores of females from which to choose, and all without the penalty of having to guide this damned old wagon along the winding maze of mud tracks he was now on. At least he had been lucky so far; he had barely covered half a mile when the black- garbed hunter emerged from the bushes and hailed him. The girl he had caught lay securely trussed not twenty yards from the track, and between them they hefted her up and carried her over to the wagon. The hunter thanked Daniel, pressed a shilling coin into his hand as a reward, and set off back towards the Hall.

An hour later, however, and he still had not added to his cargo. He passed two other hunters, but neither of them had so far made a 'kill', and after giving him vague salutes of acknowledgement, they had disappeared back into the woods to continue their quest. Daniel peered up through the trees towards the sky, noting the position of the sun. The afternoon was drawing towards evening now. Soon it would be time to consider running down any loose bird-girls himself, not that they could come to any harm or get into any mischief from being left out all night. As his cousin had said, they would make their way back soon enough when they grew thirsty and hungry, but the more of them that were returned for the evening festivities, the better it would go down with the guests. It would also save Adam the trouble of preparing too many substitutes from amongst the girls who had been left behind.

He sighed, drew back on the traces to signal the old horse to stop, and dropped lightly down onto the grass beside the track. Why waste all this time looking for something when you had it in your hands already? These stupid nobs who spent their time running around after a bunch of dim-witted wenches dressed up in feathers would scarcely know whether they were fucking something they had caught themselves, or whether they had their cocks inside a girl who had spent most of the afternoon chained to a wall in one of the holding pens. But then again, if he missed one that had been caught and trussed up already, she would hardly be able to make her own way back. Then it would be up to the keepers to scour the grounds for her and Grayling would be down on Adam like a ton of stone blocks. Daniel sighed again. He would continue on, as he knew he must, but first no one would blame him for taking a short rest. And the girl in the back of the wagon would probably be grateful to have the use of her legs again, even if only for a few minutes, and at the expense of having them wrapped around him while he ploughed her furrow.

He saw her as he was about to lower the tailboard. She wandered slowly out from between the trees away to his right and began walking unsteadily towards him. He leaned against the wagon and grinned, for even at this distance there was no mistaking those magnificent mounds bobbing up and down before her. It was the girl who had arrived with Sam's last but one consignment, the girl all the lads had nicknamed Titty Kitty. By all accounts she was quite something, and she had been tamed and trained quicker than most. But such had been her popularity, in particular the demand for those magnificent melons, that Daniel had so far not had the opportunity to sample her for himself.

And now here she was, all neatly parcelled up in her bird costume, limping slightly and obviously no longer interested in running. He looked over at the back of the wagon and at the bird-girl lying hunched in her tight and excruciatingly uncomfortable bondage. 'Just you lie still a bit longer,' he said, 'while I catch our little friend over there, and then I'll loosen the ties on your legs for a bit while I loosen a few things for her.' He chuckled at his quick wit, and taking up one of the coils of thin cord from inside the wagon began walking towards the approaching Kitty.

Adam Portfield stood motionless in the doorway of the barn room for a few moments considering the scene before him while listening intently for any sound of movement from outside. The girl, Sarah, lay on her back, her legs open, her hands between her thighs. She was groaning quietly, but her eyes were closed and she appeared not to be aware of his presence. In fact, Adam realised as he stepped further into the chamber, she did not seem aware of anything at all except herself.

Leaving her for a moment, he went and knelt beside the prone figure of Ross. The young handler was completely unconscious, but not dead; Adam's expert probing quickly established a pulse in his neck. He frowned. It was possible Ross had been careless and the girl had managed to hit him with something while his back was turned. Yet even if it was she who felled him, Adam doubted she had been the one to truss him as securely as he was now. The knots showed expertise, and the manner in which his bound ankles had been drawn back up to double his legs behind him, and then tied off to the cords about his wrists, suggested the person responsible knew a thing or two about immobilising prisoners.

He took his knife from his belt and quickly sliced through the web of lashings. Ross was unlikely to regain consciousness for a good while yet, but at least when he did so he would not have the added discomfort of recovering circulation. With a grunt of annoyance, Adam stood up again and moved over to the girl.

Despite her shorn head and the grimy stains now streaking her face, he recognised her. This was the girl the women had taken from the coach the other night, the prim and proper little miss who had protested her abduction in such haughty tones. A virgin upon her arrival, she had been passed on to Ross for her induction into the world of slavery. Well, Adam mused, it seemed the lad had done a good job, for not only was she still completely unaware of him looming over her, she was now steadily masturbating. Her sex was swallowing her fingers and her clitoris was jutting from between them, shining a deep pink.

He scratched the side of his jaw and took a half pace backwards. Yes, she would fetch a fine price all right if this exhibition were anything to judge Ross's progress by. In less than forty-eight hours she had transformed from frozen maiden into *this*. He grinned, but then quickly frowned again.

Later perhaps, he told himself firmly. First there were things to be done and questions to be answered. If the girl wasn't responsible for Ross's predicament, then someone else was, and that someone would hardly have happened upon the pair by accident. Adam's gaze scoured the room and quickly lit upon what he needed. With a muttered oath, he strode quickly to the corner and picked up the water bucket.

Kitty made no attempt to resist as Daniel turned her about and looped the cord around her wrists, drawing her winged arms behind her back and securing them with a quick knot. Turning her again, he placed a hand carefully on each of her exposed breasts, and then gently squeezed them so her bell-hung nipples protruded from between his thumbs and forefingers.

'Pretty titties indeed.' He shook them so the bells tinkled quietly.

From behind her mask Kitty stared back into his eyes, her breathing steady and noisy through the nostril openings, her mouth distended by the tightly buckled gag.

'Time nearly to take you back, my gorgeous little fucky bird,' Daniel chuckled. Kitty's gaze was unblinking. 'But first,' he continued, reaching around her to locate the buckle that held the gusset strap in place, 'I think we've got time for a little stuffing of our own.' The strap fell away to hang between them and the front dildo slid easily out between Daniel's fingers. He held it up. The leather covering glistened in the greenish light filtering through the foliage high above them. 'Oh dear,' he chuckled, 'you *do* seem to have got yourself into a state.' He let the thing fall to the ground and reached back between her thighs, feeling her warmth and the wetness that had seeped past the strap. He sniffed, smelling her arousal. 'Down we go,' he whispered, grasping her upper arms and pushing her backwards.

Obligingly, Kitty sank to the ground and lay back, immediately opening her legs for him, her large breasts spreading upon her chest among the gaudy feathers.

'More than a mouthful there, I think,' Daniel muttered as he tugged at his belt. 'And a nice warm scabbard for my sword, I reckon.' His breeches were about his knees and his penis already fully erect. Without further ado, he sank to his knees and leaned over her, supporting his weight with his left arm while with his right hand he grasped his shaft and guided the head of it to her opening. He lowered his head further, drawing her right nipple into his mouth as at the same time he began to enter her.

Instantly, Kitty's back arched and her legs twined themselves about his thighs, seeking to pull him in deeper with a ferocious urgency. Daniel sucked harder, pushing steadily and savouring the steady entrance rather than thrusting quickly. 'Lovely,' he breathed, and began to pump in and out of her, letting himself rest squarely upon the cushion of her soft breasts. There was no tremendous hurry; after he came quickly during this first round, there should still be time to enjoy a second, more relaxed coupling before it was time to get her into the cart.

The explosion came quickly, but when it did it was not the orgasmic release he was expecting. Instead, bright and fiery lights erupted before his eyes, and there was just time enough for Daniel to register the searing pain spreading from the back of his head before a deep, velvety blackness rose up to claim him.

'You're lying to me, slut!' Adam Portfield roared. 'And I won't have slaves thinking they can lie to me!' The whip snaked out, cracking as it wrapped about Sarah's naked and sweat-drenched body.

She screamed, jumping in the air and trying to skip away across the floor to escape the next blow. 'No,' she wailed, turning around and backing herself up against the wall, her hands held protectively over her breasts. 'No please, master, I swear it! I don't know who they were! They were just two men and a lad!'

'Liar.' Adam's whip whistled across the gap between them. This time only the tip caught her, but it was a deliberate aim and a small red line erupted just beneath her navel.

Sarah shrieked as she fell to her knees, clutching the injured area with both hands and lowering her shaven head in an attitude of submission. 'Please,' she wailed, sobbing in terror. 'I didn't know them. I don't know them.'

Adam paused, studying her critically. Perhaps she was telling the truth. But why would three men, or rather two men and a lad, come here deep inside the Grayling estate and just happen upon her and Ross? And why would they then, having dealt with Ross so efficiently, leave the wench here alone? Perhaps they intended to return for her later? He pursed his lips, concentrating. He was alone with her now, unarmed except for his knife and the whip, and if there were indeed intruders wandering the woods, it might be a bad move on his part to try to get back to the house, or to find help from the main barn. Alone, he could probably make a break through the trees and keep ahead and clear of any strangers, but that would mean leaving the girl behind, and if they did manage to return and take her, that could bring all manner of trouble. She had been unlawfully abducted, not bought cheaply in the slave auctions like the majority of the girls. If he took her with him, it would slow his progress as well as hand her over to the unknown intruders on a plate if they caught up with him in the open.

He needed to know more, to wait and consider and not rush his decision. The barn was a solid building, the only windows small and set high beneath the eaves, and the outer door was solid, not easily broken through. The place had never been locked from the outside since it was first built, but there was a timber bar for securing it from within which had never been used. He peered sideways at Ross. The younger man still lay motionless, so it was unlikely Adam could count on help from him in the near future. For the moment he was on his own and that left only one sensible option.

'Don't move!' he barked at the still kneeling Sarah. 'Stay exactly where you are.' He wheeled around and strode out and along the passageway to the outer door. With a sigh of relief, he saw the locking bar was there propped up in the corner. He peered outside cautiously. The ground in front of the barn was deserted but the screen of trees some fifty yards away now seemed somehow darker and more menacing.

Without further delay, Adam dropped the whip to the ground and sprang forward, dragging the first door closed, his heart pounding both from the effort of swinging the heavy timbered structure and from the fear that at any moment the intruders might return and spring upon him. The door banged hollowly against the top frame and already he had seized its mate. The hinges groaned a little from lack of use, but he had it moving now. The door slammed closed with a dull, booming thud, and then the bar was in his hands, dropping solidly into the locking slots. He stepped back, breathing hard but flushed with success.

Whoever was out there, if indeed they still were, would not be getting inside in a hurry. He had bought himself time, time to question the girl more thoroughly and time for his, and Ross's, absence to be noticed. It was beginning to grow dark outside. Darkness could be his ally as well as his enemy. If he was not back at the house, or at the main barn, within an hour of nightfall, others would start to worry. Daniel would know he should have been back, as he always was, before the evening festivities began, and they would send men out to search for him, especially when they realised Ross was also missing.

'Let's find ourselves a lantern or two first,' he muttered, stooping to retrieve the discarded whip. 'We'll get ourselves some nice cosy light, and then we'll find out just how much the little slut really knows.'

Paddy Riley stood back against the nearest tree, musket at the ready, as Sean bent over their latest victim binding his wrists and ankles. A few feet away, Kitty lay on her back moaning softly into her gag.

'This is getting feckin' ridiculous, Paddy,' Sean complained, tying off the final knot with a fierce jerk. 'We're collecting these buggers like they're going out of fashion.' He peered back over his shoulder, his eyes all but hidden by the black mask he now wore. 'I make that two girls and two fellows here, plus one more girl and one more fellow we've left back at that barn.'

'Well, we'll gag this one and leave him here,' Paddy replied. 'I'd leave the two wenches, too, but I'd not be able to face meself in the morning if we didn't at least try to get them out of this hellhole of a place. At least we've got ourselves some transport now,' he added, trying to sound cheerful.

'Yeah, and look at the size of it,' Sean said derisively. 'Me mammy used to push a wheelbarrow not much short of that thing. And that nag looks half dead, I reckon.'

'He looks it, and I feel it,' Paddy said wearily. 'Now, quit blabbering and let's get your man there off the trail and into the bushes, then we can get our wench up and into the wagon and try to get it turned around and head back towards the barn. It'll be a squeeze, but I reckon we can fit the third girl and the wee lad in the back. You and me can sit up front. That way, dressed as we are, anyone sees us they'll think we're just going about our rightful business, or what passes for rightful business in this place.' He looked up at the sky between the overhanging branches. 'It'll be dark in another half an hour, or thereabouts. That means we'll have to watch ourselves until we get onto a wider track, but it also means we can probably get right up to the guard the lad says they keep on the main gate and jump the buggers before they know what's happening.'

'The boy reckons there's usually four or five of them,' Sean reminded him, standing up and stretching his back. 'And there's just the two of us,' he added unnecessarily.

Paddy stifled a yawn and lowered his musket. 'But *we're* proper soldiers, Sean my boy. And apart from having the element of surprise, as my old captain used to keep going on about, I reckon I've got an idea of how we can level up those odds a bit. Let's get back to the barn where we left the boy and I'll show you a little trick I picked up in the days when we were still fighting Charlie boy's royalists.'

'Now then, you lying little whore,' Adam growled, 'let's see if we can't get to the truth of the matter.' He finished buckling the second ankle strap and straightened up, stepping back to take in the full picture of helplessness he had created. Ross was most certainly, he thought, a very inventive young man.

Sarah sat perched upon a high stool to the back of which had been attached a sturdy upright post. It was a similar construction to the device upon which Ross had secured her earlier, except the seat was plain and much higher, and the cross member for securing her wrists was only at waist level. This time her legs were dragged back and secured at the ankles to a second cross member a foot or so below the other, forcing her thighs wide apart and fully displaying her open sex. It was a most uncomfortable position in itself, without any additional punishment being inflicted, and Adam could see how an hour or so in the clutches of this particular seat might reduce even the most stubborn slave to something approaching obedience.

On the bench at the rear of the room, however, he had already spied something else which, when added to the muscle-wracking discomfort of Sarah's current position, he was more than confident would expedite matters nicely. As he stepped over and picked up the artificial phallus to examine it more closely, he knew he was right. The instrument had been carved with exquisite care from what appeared to be ebony, and was, he thought, a work of art produced by a craftsman of the highest calibre. It measured a good twelve inches in length with a diameter of perhaps a quarter of that, and its entire surface was covered in spiked protuberances whose points had just barely been rounded off. The insertion of such a weapon would be a far from pleasant experience for the victim, and as he walked back and held it up before Sarah's face, the horror in her eyes told him she understood this even better than he did.

'Now then, missy,' he sneered, turning the polished and knobbed surface over and over in his hands to toy with her terror, 'let's see how that hungry little pussy of yours likes this as a friend.' He leaned forward and extended the tip of the shaft until it was nestling between the parted lips of her sex.

Instinctively, Sarah tried to draw back, but the rigidity of her bondage made it impossible for her to move more than the merest fraction of an inch. 'Please,' she whimpered, tears forming in her eyes and her lower lip quivering with terrified anticipation. 'Master, no.'

'But yes, I think.' Adam began pushing the dreadful thing into her.

She gave another little shriek and her eyes rolled up away from the sight of what was being done to her.

He pressed still further and the first knobs began to dig into her tender inner flesh. He saw a sudden change of expression on her face, wondered for just a brief moment if the bitch was actually beginning to enjoy this torture, and then realised she was looking past him. It took another split second for the significance of this to register, and then he was turning, but it was already too late. He lifted one arm defensively, opening his mouth to yell out defiantly, but the length of timber in the lad's hands was heavy and swinging in a fast arc. The last thing Adam Portfield heard in the instant before the makeshift club shattered the side of his skull was the high-pitched curse that issued from his youthful assailant's lips.

It took several minutes for Paddy and Sean to turn the little wagon around. The soft soil away from the path meant they were forced to unhitch the elderly horse and drag the vehicle around by hand, but at last they completed the task, and after another minute or so spent regaining their breath, they led the docile animal back between the shafts.

'If they try chasing after us,' Sean quipped, 'then my money's not going to be on us. This bugger's got two speeds, and the fastest of them is slow, for sure.'

'Well, if my little plan works out,' Paddy said, 'then they won't be after chasing us for quite a bit, so will you stop worrying and just get those damned hitches fastened? It's getting so dark here I can barely see me hand in front of me face now, and it's a good half mile back before the track gets any wider than it is here.'

'Well, I'm already done my side,' Sean stepped back a pace and looked up at the rapidly darkening sky. 'Maybe one of us should walk ahead,' he suggested, 'and yes, I know, it'll be me 'cos you're the bloody sergeant.'

'Privileges of rank,' Paddy said, chuckling. 'But I don't mind if you'd rather drive. My arse never did much appreciate a hard wooden seat, and this trail is about as rough as any a man would ever want to drive over.'

'Well, and aren't you just the... holy shit!' Sean's reply was interrupted in midstream as the dark figure suddenly rushed out of the trees and leapt for Paddy. The creature flew straight for the throat of the older soldier, screeching and spitting, the last of the daylight glinting dully on outstretched talons, and only Paddy's soldier's instincts allowed him to twist sideways and duck clear at the last moment. He rolled away but then was up again in an instant, his hand reaching for the bayonet knife that hung from his belt beneath the black jerkin.

Sean's initial surprise had also given way to action, and now he was fumbling beneath his own jerkin, grabbing at the pistol, which caught for a moment in the leather folds. The horse, sensing something unexpected and dangerous, whinnied loudly and made a half-hearted attempt to rear up. The wagon rolled backwards a few feet, and the snarling beast collided heavily with the front wheel.

'Holy shit!' Sean heard Paddy cry as the black silhouette whirled around to face him. 'Jeez, it's a bloody girl! I—'

The rest of his words were drowned out by the crack of Sean's pistol discharging, and the flash from the muzzle momentarily blinded both men. There was a scream of agony in the darkness followed by a shout, this time decidedly female, and then there was silence, broken only by the snuffled breathing of the startled horse and the gentle creaking of the wagon as the poor beast shifted his weight forward again.

'Paddy?'

'Yeah, I'm all right.'

'What the feck was that?'

'How the hell should I know?' There was a brief pause. 'Some sort of... well, I wouldn't like to say. It was a woman, I think, but she had claws and fangs and eyes like burning coals.' Paddy emerged from around the front of the horse and Sean saw he was breathing heavily. 'For a minute there I thought I was facing a bloody banshee,' he said, his voice betraying his shock. 'Did you see those bloody talons, man?'

'I think I hit it, whatever it was,' Sean replied, trying to ignore the tremor in his own voice.

Paddy stepped up to him, and clapped him on the shoulder. 'I think you did, too,' he said, 'and I thank you for it. For a minute there I thought the she-devil had me, but she ran off when you fired. I'm not sure whether... hey, listen up a minute.' He stopped, turning his head.

'What?' Sean began, but then he too heard it, a low moan of pain, most definitely female.

'Over there,' Paddy said, pointing. 'I thought I heard something when that demon creature ran off. Quick man, there's a woman there, and she sounds like she's hurt!'

Harriet shivered in the rapidly cooling night air and almost stumbled over an exposed tree root as Silas Grout led her across the green. The sun had disappeared over an hour ago. She had tried praying during the interim, but she found that words would not come. Her faith, it seemed, had deserted her.

Grout had come for her at last, the men forming the guard about her painful perch moving aside for him, and she tried to steel herself to meet her end with as much dignity as her nakedness and terrible bondage would permit. As the pole was withdrawn from between her back and elbows, she stared across the green to where the noose was silhouetted darkly beneath the overhanging bough. It would be quick, at least, if Grout was to be believed, and in one way her death would be a welcome release from her agonising humiliation at the hands of these evil men.

She closed her eyes, tried to swallow, and braced herself for the final walk. Yet it was not to the execution tree Grout led her but back towards the darkened church. And as she stumbled along at his side she realised there were no other people about - no expectant crowd waiting to see her die. Instead, as they drew closer to that section of the graveyard wall which stood highest of all on either side of the gate, her eyes made out the shapes of two horses in the shadows... and a figure dressed all in black who she knew, without having to look more closely, was none other than Jacob Crawley.

'You spread the story as I instructed?' Crawley's voice in the darkness cut like a rusted rapier blade.

Harriet shivered again.

'I did, yes,' Grout replied. 'There was a little discontentment, but not much, just as you predicted, master. Most have now gone away to their beds, or down to the inn, to await the dawn entertainment they're now expecting.'

'Good.' Crawley coughed to clear his throat, and then spat fiercely against the wall. 'And you've ordered two men to guard the wagon back there? If this bitch has any friends left, they may think they can help her by destroying the scaffold.'

'They'll not get near it,' Grout said firmly. 'Those ignorant fools are not so ignorant as not to know they'll not get paid if they make any stupid mistakes at this stage.'

'Then the sooner we do this, the better,' Crawley announced. 'Lift the whore up onto my horse. She can ride before me as a shield, just in case the witch and the whelp think they can try taking pot shots. You stay behind me, Silas, but have both your pistols at the ready, primed and cocked.'

Confused at this latest turn of events, Harriet tried to clear her thoughts as she was hefted into the air and thrown astride the saddle of the first horse. A moment later, Crawley mounted behind her and she felt him pressing into her back, his weight pushing her forward until the raised pommel at the front of the saddle was digging into her unprotected sex. She moaned, and heard the witchfinder chuckle close to her ear.

'Keeping your legs spread till the very end?' he taunted. 'Well, when we've taken care of your crone of a grandmother and that snot-nosed miller's boy, maybe we'll spread them a bit further for you one last time.'

Harriet squirmed, trying to ease her position, but the effort simply added not only to her general discomfort but also to the sudden heat the initial friction against the hard leather saddle inexplicably aroused in her. She blinked, peering about her and trying to make some sense of all this. Grandmother and then miller's boy, Crawley had said. That had to mean Matilda's grandmother, Hannah, and James Calthorpe, who had been keeping company with Matilda of late, according to village gossip. There had been talk in the crypt of a tithe - ransom by any other name - and although Harriet had only caught snatches of discussions between Crawley and Grout, she guessed that the witchfinder had offered Hannah her granddaughter's life in exchange for money. There had long been rumours that the old woman had a hidden fortune left to her by her father, even though she lived most frugally in her tiny cottage. Considering this, Harriet began to understand.

Wickstanner had apparently brought in Crawley because of allegations that Matilda was a witch, or at best a heretic, possibly because she had rebuffed his amorous advances. Crawley had come, but not for this reason; the man was a fraud and a charlatan, his principle crusade not to save damned souls but to extort money. Hannah must have realised this and at first refused to pay up (this much had also come from snippets of conversation Harriet overheard in the crypt) but when it became clear that Crawley was not bluffing, she had been forced to concede.

Now Crawley and his henchman were taking her to meet Hannah and James, presumably having arranged a rendezvous for the exchange, or so the old woman must have been led to believe. Crawley, however, obviously had no intention of honouring his side of the bargain. She, Harriet - Matilda as far as anyone but Jane Handiwell was concerned - was to be his protective shield, and Silas Grout would shoot the unsuspecting couple down in cold blood. After that, with Hannah's gold safely in hand, Crawley would indeed finally kill Harriet. The villagers had evidently been told the postponed execution would now take place at dawn, but with his mission already accomplished, she doubted Crawley would bother allowing her to live that long. A fatal shot from a musket could be attributed to the old woman, or to young James Calthorpe, and silence the only witness to his treachery. Harriet was certain that her chances of seeing even the first glimmerings of another day were remote as Crawley kicked his mount into a trot and headed it out across the now deserted village green.

Paddy Riley was not a man usually at a loss for words, but the scene that greeted them when Toby Blaine finally responded to his soft call and admitted them into the barn came close to leaving him speechless.

'He was trying to get the lady to tell who we were,' Toby explained, pointing calmly at the second form lying sprawled alongside the still unconscious first man. 'Don't worry, he's dead all right,' Toby added as Paddy moved to examine the corpse. 'I whacked him with that big lump of wood there. He was hurting her bad, so I just hit him as hard as I could. I didn't mean to kill him, but I reckon he was a pretty wicked sod anyway.'

'Aye, that he was, I reckon,' Paddy murmured. He looked across to where Sarah now sat huddled against one wall, her nakedness covered by a piece of sacking. Her eyes were open but they did not seem to be focused, and he doubted she was really aware of much of what was happening around her.

'She's Miss Harriet's cousin, Sarah,' Toby said, following Paddy's eyes. 'I don't think she's feeling very well, but I sat and talked to her for a bit while we waited. Lots of what she was saying I didn't really understand, but she told me her name, and that she was taken from the coach the other night. And,' he added, his eyes gleaming, 'you'll never guess what else she said, though I'm not sure whether it's true or just her rambling on.' He paused for effect. 'What she said was that they weren't highwaymen at all, but highway *women!* Would you believe it?'

'I reckon I'd believe just about anything right now,' Paddy retorted. He turned to Sean. 'Nip back out to the wagon and bring in that other wench. I've a mind I know where I've seen her before, but young Toby here can tell us for sure. If I'm right, then the sooner we get out of here the better, though I'm doubting what we have to tell will be welcome news to Master Handiwell.'

'This was my father's,' Hannah Pennywise said, and straightened up with some difficulty in the corner where she had removed the small section of flooring. She carefully pulled the layers of sacking away from the object she had retrieved from the hidey-hole to reveal a curious pistol-like weapon. It had a handle and a flintlock mechanism and was small enough to be held in one hand, but the barrel was unlike anything James Calthorpe had ever seen on any weapon other than a full-sized blunderbuss. It was trumpet-shaped, and across the muzzle measured a good five to six inches.

'It hasn't been fired these past fifty years,' Hannah went on, 'so only the gods know what will happen when the trigger is pulled next. Do you know anything about this sort of thing, lad?'

James held out a hand and carefully took the weapon from her. 'I think it's a very early flintlock mechanism,' he ventured a dubious guess. 'Is it loaded?'

'Hardly, but there's powder in a pot on the shelf somewhere, and a bag of small balls I've been using as a doorstop since my pa died.'

'Let's see how the flint is then.' James raised the cumbersome pistol, cocked the hammer and pulled back on the trigger. There was a rasping clack of metal followed by a bright shower of sparks. 'Astonishing,' he muttered. 'It looks like it'll still work, but to be honest, I've not the slightest idea how something like this should be loaded.'

'Ah, well I have,' Hannah assured him, 'so you just pass it back over here and hand me down that black pot above the bed there. I doubt there's enough powder for more than one decent shot, but then I also doubt whether there'll be time to reload for a second go anyway.'

'If that thing delivers as bad as it looks,' James muttered, 'I doubt there'll be much need of a second shot. The only trouble as I see it,' he added nervously, 'is that something like that is hardly very selective.'

'That it ain't, and it also ain't much good beyond about fifteen paces, but close up anything within several feet either side is like to be ripped apart.'

'And Matilda is going to be right in the line of fire,' James pointed out.

Hannah sniffed, and took the pot of powder he passed her. 'Don't think I don't know that,' she said, 'but then beggars can't be choosers, and apart from that other pistol, this is all we've got. So, you take the other gun and I'll have this one. I expect you can shoot straighter than I ever could, let alone now I'm an old biddy, so it'll be up to you. Try to drop that black bastard Crawley first. If I'm any judge, he'll have Matilda close to him to hide behind. If he's got his other man with him I'll try to get a clear shot at him, so you'll have to be quick and try not to miss. There won't likely be any second chances.'

'And what if he has more than the one man with him?' James asked.

Hannah was carefully tipping powder down the gaping black muzzle, and didn't respond.

'It looked like he had several others working for him from what I could see back at the green. Two pistols won't be much good then, even if that thing might take a couple of men out in one shot.'

'He'll only have the one,' Hannah replied, a note of total certainty in her voice. She looked up from her task to smile grimly. 'Those other buggers are only in this for a handful of whatever he's promised them, mark my words, and Crawley won't want any witnesses this night, not if he's planning what I think he's planning.'

'But if we know he's planning to double-cross us, and he'll be using Matilda as some sort of shield, why are we even thinking of being there to meet him?'

'Because we ain't got a lot of choice from where I'm sitting,' Hannah snapped. 'If we don't turn up by the three elms at the appointed hour, he'll just take her back and hang her straight off. And anyway, the fact that we're expecting the bastard to play dirty gives us that little edge *he* won't be expecting. Now quit your mithering and get down under this bed. There should be a couple of coils of rope under there somewhere. If we hurry, there should be just enough time for us to arrange a little diversion for Master Crawley and his friend.'

Matilda Pennywise groaned through her gag as she was finally lifted down from the wagon. She could barely stand, and but for the support of the man called Sean she would have collapsed to her knees. Nearly two hours bound in one position, even though they had cut the cords about her legs and ankles, had left her feeling stiff and sore, and now she had to be half carried into the barn.

The events of the day were blurred in her mind, but she remembered everything clearly enough. First she was dressed in one of the ridiculous bird costumes and herded together with a group of other similarly dressed girls, and then they had been sent off into the woods to run around as sport for those sinister looking black-garbed hunters. Tired and covered in tiny scratches from all the brambles, she had managed to avoid capture for what seemed like an eternity, only to be scooped up at the last and trussed like a chicken bound for the oven. She was then dumped into the little wagon where she bounced about as the driver apparently went in search of further quarry. After that there had been a sudden flurry of action in which something happened to the original driver, and then a second girl had been deposited in the wagon with her, a girl with the largest breasts Matilda had ever seen. Then there was more trouble outside, some sort of fight followed by a pistol shot. She heard raised voices and some talk about a woman being hurt before the two men lifted yet another female into the now crowded wagon, a woman dressed like the male hunters except she wasn't wearing a mask, and her face was all too familiar to Matilda. The innkeeper's daughter had sat jammed into a corner of the wagon, her hands bound behind her, her mouth stuffed with a gag, glaring across at her with undisguised hatred. Matilda, who wondered why these men had chosen to remove Kitty's gag and not her own, glared back at her in turn until fatigue finally fell heavy upon her eyelids, and she drifted off into a doze until the wagon finally stopped at the barn.

She still had no idea what was happening, or who these newcomers were, but the man Sean, at least, seemed to be taking care to handle her gently as he helped her into one of the inner chambers.

'Bugger me!'

Matilda's head jerked up at the sound of the youthful voice, and she found herself staring at Toby Blaine. For a moment she thought his outburst was due to the fact that he had recognised her, but then she realised her features were still hidden beneath the feathered hood and that he had merely been surprised by her garish and bizarre appearance.

'Stop staring, lad,' Sean said quietly. 'Ain't the lady's fault, whoever she is. Just make a bit of room there and help her down. She looks like she could use a drink, too. See if you can get that thing off her head and get her a drop of water, there's a good lad. I'm going to fetch the other two in and I'll wager they've a healthy thirst on them by now as well.'

Oona pushed her way through a thicket of brambles and threw herself onto the grass, alternately whimpering and growling and trying to turn her head far enough to get a look at the wound on her shoulder. She could smell the blood and feel the burning pain where the ball had torn through her furry jerkin, ripping the flesh beneath it, but she could not tell the extent of the damage. At least she could still move her arm.

She rolled over onto her back and sat up, staring down at the gleaming claws tipping her fingers. They made it impossible for her to probe the wound without inflicting further injury, and the rigidity of the glove, as well as the intricacy of the fastenings holding them over her hands, made it equally impossible for her to remove them unaided. She snorted in anger and frustration, and shook her head like a mad dog in an effort to clear it of the whirling red and grey mists that always seemed to rise before her eyes whenever she attempted to think straight.

She was accustomed to pain. The handlers here were never sparing in their use of the whip, and she could vaguely remember back to earlier days when women had used canes on her, beating her savagely day and night until she thought she would prefer to die than face another dawn. It had all been so unfair, for it was not her fault. She had not asked to grow into the grotesque creature that had emerged from her original girlish body as she entered into adulthood. Oona could hardly remember those innocent childish times now, yet she knew she had been happy, and that she had lived in a large house and worn soft clothes and slept in a soft bed. But she had been different, and her difference had appalled and frightened people she thought loved her and would protect her. They had beaten her. They had cast her out. They had sold her to traders just to get her out of their sight. And the traders had beaten her and made her into a wild and savage animal, tormenting and then playing with her until the object of so much horror and curiosity arose from its slumber and displayed itself in all its blatant lust.

Her eyes narrowed as these memories whirled through her head. She would never forget the way they brought her here, dressed her as she was now, and called her 'dog-girl' and 'bitch-hound'. They had forced their various tonics into her, and there had been times when she believed herself mad and that she truly was a wild dog. She barked and yelped and bounded after whatever they told her to chase. She fell upon women whose scent drove her to the verge of insane lust, a lust only abated when she could mount them like bitches and plunge her hated and demanding shaft deep inside them, pounding until she sprayed her barren seed into their squirming bodies.

Slowly, Oona rose to her feet. Her head was beginning to throb, as it always did just before they gave her her morning and evening meals. She peered down at herself. Sure enough, the throbbing member was fully awake and demanding its needs be answered. She reached down and gently touched its length with one talon, shivering as she did so, and then raised her head and sniffed the night air speculatively.

The log was a section of a large branch three to four feet in length and split in two where a smaller branch had been growing off to one end. There were four additional projections much smaller in diameter that had all been broken off short, either by the original fall or in the time since then.

'I had young Toby Blaine, and a couple of his friends, drag this over for me back in the spring,' Hannah said. 'I found it lying in the woods a week or two before. You can see where someone's chopped a bit away at one end, but it was a tad rotten, so they left it. It would have done for firewood though, if I could have bribed one of the boys to chop it for us.'

'I'd have done it for you, if you'd had Matilda ask,' James asserted.

In the near darkness, Hannah grinned. 'I know, and that was my next move. But the thing is, young Jamie, do you reckon you can carry it?'

James walked around the piece of timber, studying it.

'It probably weighs about forty to fifty pounds,' she added. 'My pa used to bring home lumps like this on his shoulder all the time.'

'How far do you want me to carry it?' James asked. He stooped and knelt, reaching beneath the twisted limb to test its weight.

'As far as the three elms, where else do you think?' Hannah snapped irritably. 'You think I've got time to worry about lighting fires in the cottage right now?'

'Well, Mistress Pennywise,' James replied quietly, 'perhaps if you told me exactly what it was you were planning, I'd have a better idea of what was expected of me. Whether you've got magical powers as people say, or not, I most certainly haven't, so I can't read minds.'

'You wouldn't want to read mine, young man,' Hannah retorted, yet her expression softened and she smiled gently at him. 'But you're right,' she said, and speaking quietly and rapidly, she outlined the plan she had come up with.

James listened in silence, nodding now and then, and then he too smiled. 'Yes,' he said at last. 'Yes, that would most certainly come as something of a surprise to Master Crawley. But the question is, can we make it work?'

'No,' Hannah replied sombrely. 'The question is, can we afford not to? And the answer, my lad, ain't going to come to us standing here. Nothing ventured, nothing gained, as they say.'

Jane stared defiantly at Toby Blaine and at the two troopers, but her outward defiance masked an inner turmoil that had begun the moment Paddy and Sean removed her mask. It now reached a boiling point as she was confronted with young Toby, who identified her without any trouble, confirming Paddy's earlier suspicion as to her identity. A few moments later, however, things became infinitely worse from her point of view when the bird-girls were unmasked and it was revealed that one of them was, despite her lack of hair, most unmistakably Matilda.

'You're sure, lad?' Paddy asked when Toby had stopped gawping long enough to tell the men who she was.

Matilda, her jaw aching from being gagged for hours, glared fiercely at the Irishman. 'Of course he's sure, you idiot! He's known me and my grandmother for as long as I've lived in the village, and that's more than two years now.'

'But...?' Paddy looked from Matilda, to Toby, to Jane and back to Matilda again. 'You'll have to pardon my ignorance, miss, but I was under the impression you was the girl that witchfinder fellow had in the church, at least that was the talk while I was in the village.'

'She was,' Toby interrupted. 'I was watching when that Crawley and his men took her. Wickstanner was with them, and he read out something from a piece of paper.'

'Yes,' Matilda confirmed, her face grim with tension at the memory, 'that was me sure enough, and it was me he was intending to hang, but then *she* took me from the crypt. There's a passageway leading out from it into the graveyard, and she brought me here. I thought they'd come to save me, but...' she shrugged, looked pointedly down at herself and then across at Kitty, who was listening to the exchange with a vaguely uninterested look on her face. 'Well, as you can see, I was hardly rescued. The one good thing was that at least here nobody was threatening to hang me.'

'You want to try explaining any of this?' Paddy demanded, rounding on Jane. 'No, I thought not,' he snapped when she just stared at him. 'Well, I think you'll have some explaining to do to your daddy soon enough, but meantime, if you're not you, Mistress Pennywise... I mean, if the girl at the church isn't you, then who in heaven's name is she?'

Matilda looked confused. 'I don't understand,' she said, 'what girl at the church? I'm here, aren't I?'

'Yes indeed, *you're* here,' Paddy confirmed, 'but they have a girl at the church they *think* is you, or at least I suppose they think she's you, though I can't for the life of me see why.'

'Because I was kept masked, with a terrible spike-thing in my mouth so I couldn't talk,' Matilda explained. 'This bitch took the mask off me in the crypt. I didn't realise they were leaving someone else in my place because it was so dark and it was all very confusing, but that's what she must have done.'

'But who?' Sean Kelly demanded. 'One of the poor girls from here, I suppose.'

'Whoever it was,' Matilda said, her eyes suddenly filling with tears, 'they'll have done for her by now. Crawley was intending to hang me at dusk, unless he's changed his mind.'

'I doubt he'll have done that,' Jane spat, breaking her silence at last. 'Like most men, he's only interested in two things, and enough gold usually means that money takes precedence over the other thing.'

'Then maybe you've got more explaining to do than I thought,' Paddy said grimly. 'If you left an innocent girl to be hanged, whether she's a slave, a servant, or whatever, that's against all the laws I ever heard of. You'll be answering to a judge for murder, missy, and I'll wager it'll be yourself that's dangling on a rope before much longer!'

'There was a time when I could shin up a tree twice as fast as that,' Hannah smiled. She peered up into the darkness of the foliage above her head, barely able to make out the pale outline of James's breeches. 'You make sure you tie that knot exactly the way I showed you now,' she warned, 'and not too tightly either, otherwise it won't slip through properly.'

'I know,' he said, his voice muffled by leaves. 'That's why I'm taking my time. I can't see a damned thing up here, so I'm having to do it by feel.'

'Now where have I heard that before?' Hannah chuckled to herself, and slowly bent over to pick up the coil of rope from which James had taken one end. Carefully, so as not to jerk at the hanging length, she began to pay it out across the grass and onto the road, peering towards the village as she did so and then looking up at the night sky. As long as the cloud cover remained, they had a chance of making this work, but if the moon broke through and Crawley saw the rope, he would guess something was up and probably rein in before reaching the appropriate spot. 'Have you done up there yet?' she called.

There was a muffled thump, followed by a whispered curse, and James emerged from the shadows. 'It's done,' he confirmed, 'just as you said.' He too now looked down the road in the direction from which Crawley would be coming. The high trees on either side meant the hard mud trail was visible for only about thirty yards before it merged with the overall blackness on either side.

'Now we move back,' Hannah instructed. 'Mind you, don't foul the rope, and we'll have to check and make sure we have it paid out straight before they get here. Have you got a kerchief, or something, preferably a light-coloured one?'

'I've got this,' James said, pulling a square of pale linen from his jacket pocket. 'What do you want me to do with it?'

'Lay it right here, in the middle of the road,' Hannah instructed. 'We'll be able to see it even in this poor light, so we'll know when that black-hearted bastard is level with the right spot.'

'Very clever,' James grunted. 'But what about Matilda? That thing could hit her too.'

'It like as not will,' Hannah agreed, 'but it's a chance we have to take. A broken bone or two will mend in time and at least she'll be alive... I hope,' she added beneath her breath as she began to walk backwards up the centre of the road, the rope trailing from her hands.

'This is a little trick I saw used by one of Charlie boy's lads outside of Bath,' Paddy explained. 'We caught the bugger alive just afterwards, and later he showed us how it was done. It's all quite simple really, and it's not likely to do much harm, but the flash is quite something, and if anyone's standing too close they'll be more interested in knocking the sparks off their clothes than in anything we'll be doing.' He held up the crudely shaped bottle into which he had been carefully pouring the lamp oil from the pitcher they found in one of the other rooms inside the barn. Now he began forcing a piece of sackcloth into the neck he had also doused in the liquid. 'We light the fuse,' he continued, 'and then throw the bugger. The glass breaks and the oil catches fire as it spreads across the ground. But this is the best bit,' he added, taking up the square of linen he had torn from his shirt. 'We'll pour about an ounce of black powder into this and bind it to the bottle with a bit of twine.'

'And when the burning oil catches it, it goes off with a big bang?' Sean surmised.

Paddy grinned. 'Actually, Sean me boy, there's not much of a bang, it's more of a big flash which scatters the burning oil in all directions. And in the darkness, I reckon the flash itself will do as much for us as any bang. If those bastards at the gate aren't expecting it, they'll be dazzled and shitting themselves. By the time they realise what's going on we can have them sorted out, and be through the gate and well on our way. Now those other two pistols you found in that end room, are they loaded yet?'

Perched ahead of Crawley, Harriet was the first to see the two figures standing in the middle of the road ahead. They were still too far away to be recognisable in the gloom, but Crawley, spotting them a moment later, hailed them regardless, confident of their identities.

'You've brought the gold, old woman?' he called out.

Harriet recognised Hannah Pennywise's crackling voice immediately. 'I've brought the half as I said in the note, Master Crawley,' she called back. 'You get the other half when I've got my granddaughter back. You have my word on that.'

'The word of a murderess and a witch?' Crawley said disdainfully. 'You expect me to accept that?'

'Take it or leave it, Jacob Crawley,' Hannah retorted. 'Besides, even if I were a murderess, it'd make me no worse than you, and probably a whole deal better.'

'Bold words, old woman.' Crawley wound an arm around Harriet's neck, and she heard the sound of a pistol being cocked behind her. 'You see well enough in this darkness, I hope, well enough to see that I have the slut Matilda right here before me?'

'Aye, I see well enough, Jacob Crawley,' Hannah responded. 'Just like your kind to hide behind a woman.'

'But not behind her skirts this time. Step forward, and show me the gold.'

'Let the girl down first.' This time it was James Calthorpe's voice.

Crawley laughed. 'You take me for a fool, do you?'

'A fool, no,' James replied.

'Then step forward with the gold.'

'Why don't *you* come forward?' Hannah suggested. 'You've got Matilda there to hide behind and your man is carrying a pistol, as well as the one I can see in your hand.'

'And I'm sure your own hands are empty beneath that shawl, Mother Pennywise,' Crawley said. 'However, even though I think the lad is also hiding a weapon behind his back, I doubt that either of you would risk hitting this bitch. Even a trained shot wouldn't chance that.'

'Then come and see your gold, Crawley,' Hannah urged. There was a blur as something arced through the air to fall with a dull chinking sound on the roadway a little ahead of Crawley's horse. Peering towards it, Harriet could see something pale lying there, but it did not look like a bag or a purse.

'We'll step back a pace, Master Crawley,' Hannah's voice came again. 'I wouldn't want you thinking we was breathing down your neck while you counted your evil gains, now would I?'

Paddy counted four figures as the little wagon steadily approached the main gate, two standing against one of the pillars and the other two squatting alongside a small fire over which a dark kettle pot had been hung from a crude spit. If they had been proper soldiers, he reflected critically, the two by the fire would have been immediately on the alert even though the slow progress of the vehicle would cause them little alarm. He glanced at the other side of the gate where the small timbered gatehouse stood, its door ajar, a light burning inside. There might be other guards within, and then again there might not, but it was best to assume the worst. 'I count four, Sean,' he whispered over his shoulder.

Behind him, crouched in the confines of the seriously overcrowded wagon, Sean held a lantern shielded by a thick piece of sacking, the flickering taper within it a more reliable source of igniting the fuse of their homemade bomb than any flint.

'There's also a gatehouse, not much more than a shed, I'd say, with a light inside. Could be there's more of them in there, but I can't tell. You see the fire?'

Sean leaned against Paddy's shoulder, taking care not to expose himself too much. 'Aye,' he confirmed, 'I see it, and I see the two by it, but I don't see the other two.'

'They're away by the left side of the gate. No, don't bother looking. I can take the pair of them easy enough once you throw that bottle towards them.'

'Not at the fire?'

'No,' Paddy said firmly. 'Those two are sitting in its light, so the flash won't affect them like it would if they were sitting in darkness. When I give the word, you lob that thing towards the gate and then put a shot into the nearest one by the fire. I'll take the second one, and then we'll see about the others. You've got three shots back there and I've got two, let's make them all count and we'll have one spare.'

'Unless there's more of the buggers in the hut,' Sean pointed out.

'Aye,' Paddy agreed, 'unless there's more of the buggers in the hut. In which case, I spy a couple of muskets propped against what I'd say is a water keg just this side of the fire there. I'll keep this nag going and you make a dive for them.'

'What if they're not loaded?'

'They ought to be.'

'But what if they're not?'

'If they're not, and there are more of the sods inside, then we're in a pile of shit, Sean Kelly, so you'd better start praying right now!'

Hannah's booby trap plan might well have worked out perfectly, however, as she remarked years later when once again telling the story of that night, if you expect the unexpected, then it no longer *is* the unexpected, and the truly unexpected when it happens will thwart the best laid plans.

It began well enough... Crawley advanced slowly, his man staying just behind him so Matilda - as Hannah and James still believed Harriet to be - remained in any line of fire the old woman and the miller's son might have. The small kerchief seemed to glow brightly in the darkness and Hannah felt certain Crawley must realise it was not the purse she had tossed towards him. But his mind was clearly on how he intended to retrieve the gold without exposing himself to a clear shot, and the only way he could achieve that end was to move past the purse while continuing to use the girl as a shield. Meanwhile, Silas Grout would dismount to collect the money. The only doubt in Hannah's mind was whether or not Crawley's greed would extend to the remaining gold, or whether once he had the half of it in his hands, along with the initial payment she had sent to the graveyard, he might decide to settle for that. If he did, both she and James would be utterly exposed.

'Are you ready?' she whispered out of the corner of her mouth.

'Ready,' came the hoarse reply, James's tremulous voice betraying his anxiety.

Hannah hoped his hand would be steadier when the moment came. Her own knuckles closed even more tightly over the stock of the miniature blunderbuss, and she prayed the old weapon would fire the first time. She peered to her right, afraid Crawley must at any moment see the rope trailing off to the side of the road. Another two yards... another yard...

Crawley seemed to sense something. She saw him pull back on the rein with the one arm, the hand in which he also clasped his pistol, his other arm still around his hostage's neck.

'Now!' she shouted.

Behind her, James pulled up the rope and jerked on it with all his might. It drew taut and up in the tree a knot slipped undone, loosing its grip on the short length of cord that held back the old stump. The branch, suspended from a second rope attached to an even higher treetop on the opposite side of the trail, swung downwards and across, gaining momentum as it went and striking the side of Crawley's horse, hitting both its leg and the girl's and knocking everything sideways.

The startled steed reared up, whinnying noisily and tipping both occupants out of the saddle. In the same moment Crawley's pistol discharged skywards with a loud report, and Hannah, stumbling forward, raised the muzzle of her father's pistol as she pulled back on the trigger. There was an even louder report and a flash of powder, followed almost immediately by a scream of pain from Silas Grout, all but drowned out by a louder shriek from his horse as the spray of small lead balls seared through both man and animal.

James was now running past Hannah, his young legs overtaking her in a few strides, and raising his own weapon towards the black figure of Crawley who was even now pulling himself upright. One good shot and it would be over, but even as James was steadying himself another silhouette suddenly came streaking out from between the trees. The figure crashed into him and sent him sprawling facedown on the road. His weapon discharged as he hit the ground, the ball hissing off into the nearby branches, and then complete pandemonium broke loose. James and the furiously spitting newcomer rolled around in the dust, horses whinnied and screamed, and Hannah stumbled and fell to her knees, a searing pain tearing across her ankle and instep. Dimly, the old woman saw the naked girl rise to her feet, tottering uncertainly with her arms still bound to her sides. Then she saw Crawley grabbing for her again as he drew a second pistol from beneath his cape and for a moment Hannah felt certain he meant to use it on the girl.

'No!' she screeched, trying to hobble forward again, but Crawley was more interested in dealing with any further threat to himself. The naked and bound prisoner was no danger to him, whereas Hannah and James might still be. He swung the weapon around, ignoring the struggle on the ground, and aimed at Hannah.

She saw the flash, the bright orange ball emerging from the barrel, and quickly fell sideways. She felt the air from the ball as it passed inches from her head just a second before she hit the ground, knocking the breath out of her old lungs, and slipped into unconsciousness.

As is inevitable with stories told over and over again through the years, the account passed down to the great grandchildren of two Irish troopers of the 7th Regiment, Southern Mounted Fusiliers, made much of the fire fight that took place that night at the gate of the Grayling estate.

In reality, the skirmish was over almost before it began. Paddy's homemade bomb ignited in front of the two guards by the gate itself with a spectacular loud whoosh of flames and sparks, and landed near enough to catch the clothing of both men in a wave of fire. In the end, it was said neither man suffered fatal injuries, but for the next few minutes they were preoccupied with rolling around on the ground in an effort to extinguish themselves. When the first man by the fire fell with a pistol ball through his shoulder, his companion was already on his feet and running into the trees, ignoring the muskets that, in any case, proved unnecessary to Paddy and Sean's cause.

There was indeed one further guard inside the hut, but he emerged with his hands held high, presumably having already seen his confederates easily vanquished, which made him more than willing to open the gate for the wagon to pass through. First making sure they had collected all the weapons, Paddy then ordered the fellow to walk ahead of them for the better part of a mile before finally releasing him, either to return to the estate, or more likely to take to his heels in another direction.

'That,' Paddy announced as the wagon rolled on its way, 'is why the English need us Irish over here to fight their fecking wars for them. About as much use as a fart in a fishing net,' he added scornfully.

Back at the inn, however, the mood was far less jocular. As they approached the *Black Drum*, they saw the courtyard was lit by several lanterns and that a row of horses stood along the hitching posts, the liveries on their saddlecloths all too familiar.

'Dragoons,' Paddy said. 'Looks like they sent men up from Portsmouth after all. Shame we've done most of their dirty work for them.'

Inside, at the small side bar, Thomas Handiwell, Captain Hart and a Lieutenant of Dragoons, a thick- set northerner named Trueman, were holding a council of war. Paddy, not wishing to cause unnecessary embarrassment in front of the two soldiers and the dragoon sergeant hovering around them, asked to speak with the innkeeper in private.

The confrontation between Thomas and Jane was a terrible scene indeed, and Paddy temporarily left father and daughter to their own devices while he sought the maid, Annie, and asked her to take charge of the two former captives. When he returned, Thomas was waiting alone outside the saloon.

'I'll thank you to keep my daughter's part in this terrible thing between us,' he said curtly, 'at least for the time being. I realise, of course, that the law must be done, but I should like some time to think.'

'Of course, sir,' Paddy replied gravely. 'After all, she's only a wee chit of a girl, when all's said and done.'

'Chit of a girl, my arse!' Thomas declared vehemently. 'She's been behind all these damned highway robberies, and on top of that, she's tried to get an innocent girl killed, albeit in place of another almost certainly innocent girl.'

'I thought the girl would have been dead by now,' Paddy said.

Thomas shook his head. 'No,' he replied. 'There was a delay for some reason and the so-called execution was postponed until morning. Lieutenant Trueman and four of his men have gone to the church to demand her release.'

'Then that's something to be thankful for, at least.'

Thomas reached inside his jacket and extracted a small leather purse, which he offered to Paddy. 'This is for you and your... err, colleague.'

Paddy looked at him diffidently. 'Most generous of you, I'm sure, sir, but Sean Kelly and me, well, we were only doing what Parliament pays us to do. And if my mind were to become, shall we say a little cloudy concerning certain events and people this night, well, I'd hate it to be thought it was because gold had fuddled it. On the other hand, sir,' he went on, 'if a man was to offer a body a good drink or two, well that could easily be excused now, couldn't it? After all, Sean and me are good and true Irishmen, and it would be an insult to the hospitality of the house to refuse an open ale tap.'

James knelt beside Hannah, holding her hand and patting her wrinkled cheek. He gave a sigh of relief when she finally opened her eyes. 'Thank God!' he breathed. 'I thought for a moment he had killed you.'

'Matilda!' the old woman croaked. 'Where is she?'

James shook his head, shamefaced. 'I don't know,' he confessed. 'I threw myself down when Crawley shot at you, and when I looked up again there was no sign of her. He was running off into the trees, but she wasn't with him, I swear it.'

'Then we must find her, and be quick about it.' Hannah struggled up into a sitting position. 'That old pistol will be of no further use this night, but the fellow you shot with it must have a weapon, if not two. Go take a look, and see if you can't do something to put that poor animal out of its misery.'

Silas Grout's mare lay where she had fallen, half across her dead master, and from the look of her it was clear that she, like Grout, would never rise again.

'Check his pockets and saddlebags for powder and ball,' Hannah called out as James began to move towards the fallen beast. 'If that black-hearted bastard is still close, we'll want to make sure we have the means at hand to dispose of him properly, once and for all.'

Harriet's instinct, when she finally picked herself up from the road amidst the shooting and shouting, was to run, and to run as fast and as far as her aching legs would carry her. Unfortunately, as she crashed through the undergrowth, blundering into brambles and trees alike in her near blind and terrified haste, she did not realise her tormentor had had the same idea. Content merely to follow her until they were well away from the road and the scene of the ambush, Crawley kept his distance. He remained out of sight until, after about half a mile, Harriet's knees finally gave way and she collapsed onto a patch of grass, whimpering in pain and fear.

Crouched behind a thick oak, he carefully reloaded his pistol, all the while listening for sounds of pursuit even though he doubted either the woman or the boy would try to come after him. The old woman had been hurt, how badly he had no idea though he thought he must have hit her, and the boy would surely wait to tend to her if she still lived.

He cursed beneath his breath. What the hell sort of weapon had the boy been carrying? The rush of air as the hail of lead passed over him and cut poor Silas to shreds had been terrifying enough in itself, and to see the mangled and bloody remains of his former aide had been something else again.

In the distance, probably in the direction from which he had come although he couldn't be sure, Crawley heard the sound of a single shot. He tensed, listening hard, but all was silent again. He finished ramming the ball down the barrel, and stood up.

The naked figure was still lying almost motionless where she had fallen, only the faint sound of sobbing betraying that she still lived. Not for much longer, he vowed, not knowing what she did about his true identity. He reached under his cape and took out the small leather purse, smiling to himself. Even in the confusion he had not forgotten his purpose for being out on that lonely road; he had scooped up Hannah's money even as he ran. He opened the drawstring and peered inside, probing with one finger. Yes, it was gold coin all right and plenty of it. He grunted in satisfaction, closed the purse and pocketed it again. Enough for a fresh horse, food, and plenty left over, and most of his own money would still be hidden beneath the ash tree on the other side of the village where he had buried it before announcing his arrival.

There would be no need to return to Leddingham again, not that he anticipated any trouble, especially not if he made it back before the old woman and the miller's boy, but it would save him having to pay off those five louts. That would more than compensate for the loss of the wagon. Without Silas it was now an encumbrance anyway, and he could replace it as well as Grout in good time. He would walk across country until he either came to another road or to a farm where he could buy horse and saddle and sufficient provisions for a couple of days, after which he would decide upon his next destination. Not Portsmouth, for there was no place for his sort of work in the bustling naval city.

No, the west country was waiting for him, with plenty of isolated villages and plenty of stupid peasants and even more stupid clergymen to aid him in his quest. But first there was the little matter of the girl to be settled. Feeling for the length of cord in the pocket of his cape, he decided she would die silently if not as quickly as originally planned. His eyes glinted in a sudden pale shaft of moonlight. Yes, the witch's whore would die, but not before he had enjoyed the warmth of her body one last time. He tucked the reloaded pistol into his belt, and began walking towards her.

Jane Handiwell sat perched on a barrel in the corner of the small cellar beneath the *Black Drum*, staring into the shadows beyond the pool of light cast by the single lantern her father had left her. She was still dressed as she had been for the hunt, apart from the mask, and she knew her appearance must have shocked the conservative Thomas almost as much as the allegations the two soldiers had made.

Allegations... she snorted. They were more than just allegations, she knew, and added to the word of the stupid Merridew girl, as well as to the fact that she was caught red-handed in the middle of Roderick Grayling's hunt, all meant she was in deep trouble. Worse still had been the news that the other Merridew bitch wasn't dead yet. Had the witchfinder discovered the truth concerning his prisoner?

Jane sighed, and shook her head. Why hadn't she just bribed one of Roderick's handlers to strangle Harriet instead of swapping her for Matilda? The scheming whore would have been dead by now and unable to testify against her. And if she had arranged for the body to be found swiftly, her father would never have been so insistent upon sending those two Irish bastards to look for her.

Highway robbery, abduction, attempted murder - they could hang her for any single one of those counts, and there would be little difficulty in proving her guilt now. On the other hand, the fact that the troopers had found Sarah on the Grayling estate meant Roderick was also implicated and would need to use all his influence. If she could get to Ellen and through Ellen to him, he would perhaps use his contacts to help her.

Yes, all was not yet lost, she reflected. Of course, things between her and her father would never be the same again, and the chances of her ever inheriting the *Drum* were now more remote than ever. Never mind, let the stupid old fool share it with his beloved Harriet, assuming she ever got around to accepting his suit. She had money of her own, hidden in the woods where no one but she could ever find it, and with that she could disappear for as long as it took the Graylings to smooth things over. All she had to do now was get out of this cellar in which Thomas had locked her, but that was unlikely to prove too great an obstacle.

She rose, and moved quietly across to the door, pressing her ear against the stout timber to listen for footsteps in the passage beyond.

Beth, her beloved little Beth, her faithful maid and bedmate these past few years... Beth had been up there on the stairs, listening as that sergeant poured out his tale to her father, and she had still been there, crouched in the shadows, when they marched her down to the cellar and locked her in. Her father had been absolutely livid, almost incapable of speech, except to promise he would be back eventually to thrash her, as he should have thrashed her years ago.

Jane barely stifled a harsh laugh. Thrash her, would he? Well, maybe he would, but she doubted it. She shuddered at the thought of baring her backside to a man with a cane, even if he was her own father, *especially* if he was her own father. But no, it would never happen, and as she continued to press her ear against the door, she knew it would not be long before Beth came for her.

Harriet did not have to open her eyes to know it was Crawley who had found her. There was something about the smell of him; an odour that pushed past even the acrid tang of the leather hood she was growing accustomed to breathing through.

She groaned, and rolled over onto her back as his boot nudged cruelly into her throbbing ribs. She opened her eyes. Past caring, she spread her legs, willing him to do his worst.

The snarling figure sprang across her vision, and for a few moments the air was filled with screeches, curses and screams of pain. A pistol shot nearly deafened her, and yet still the desperate struggle raged on. A terrible cry rent the air, followed by an awful sobbing and the pounding of booted feet. And then all went silent again. Harriet tried to roll to one side, but her strength had abandoned her, and when the terrible face appeared before her, the baleful eyes shining and huge, she knew the devil himself had determined her fate.

'He is gone.' The dreadful creature said, bending over her, and Harriet saw a flash of bright metal as the hand came down towards her. But instead of tearing into her naked flesh, it turned sideways and the back of a human hand lightly stroked her shoulder. 'Gone now,' the creature repeated. Harriet stared up into the dark face, at the frightening fangs and the lip curled back over them. 'You safe. He is gone. Not worry you now,' Oona whispered. 'Not worry any woman no more.'

'Are you drunk yet, Sean Kelly?' Paddy Riley stood in the shadow between the end of the inn and the first stable, his ale flagon held in one hand, clay pipe in the other. He had not turned around at the approaching footsteps; he had not needed to.

'Not yet, sergeant darling,' Sean said. He raised his own flagon, extending his arm in the general direction of the woods. 'Did you see the wench go, then?'

'Aye, that I did.'

'And you didn't raise the hue?'

'Didn't think it was my place, Sean lad,' Paddy muttered. 'We're off duty now, you know, else we'd be in dead trouble for drinking like this, wouldn't we?'

'Yes, I suppose,' Sean agreed. He hesitated, sipped his ale and looked at his own pipe, which had gone out. 'You think they'll catch her?'

'Maybe,' Paddy said. 'Depends how hard they look, I suppose.'

'The poor innkeeper fellow looked pretty sick at the whole thing.'

'Aye, well, he would.'

'There's talk in there of the dragoons going up to the Grayling place at first light.'

'There's always talk, Sean Kelly.'

'You don't think they will, then?'

'Oh, I'm sure they will.'

'Ah.' There was a long pause. 'You don't think it'll come to anything.'

'Maybe it will, maybe it won't.' Paddy sighed. 'All I know is, those Grayling people are money and nobility, and even though we were supposed to be fighting for democracy and the common man's rights, it'll not be in our lifetime we ever see that happen, if it ever happens at all. The Graylings of this world get away with murder because they're rich, the Crawleys get away with it because they're clever and because the Church protects its own, no matter how evil they might be. As for the innkeeper's girl, her friends at the Hall will probably help her disappear if they don't kill her. Wouldn't do for her to be standing before no court and telling what she knows now, would it?'

'And so they all get away with it?'

'Maybe,' Paddy said, 'and maybe not. As me mammy used to be so fond of telling us, God pays his debts without money.' He lifted his flagon and drained the remaining contents in one huge gulp. 'Now, what say we get ourselves back inside and take advantage of Master Handiwell's generous hospitality? This night air is growing a mite chill for my poor bones and I'm determined not to greet the dawn sober.'

With so many soldiers about, it had been impossible to get into the stable unseen and Jane had been forced to flee into the night on foot. Beth would wait until the following morning, when the dragoons left for Grayling Hall, and then bring horses and some fresh clothes to the crossroads at Petersfield, a few miles to the south west. The pair would then travel further east into Sussex and find an inn where they could lie low for a few weeks while they sent word to Grayling Hall.

Jane trudged on for nearly an hour. Finally, when she was sure she was well clear of the village, she left the road and found a grassy hollow where she could rest for a while. Her legs and feet ached and her eyes felt raw and heavy, for it had been a long day and her recent lack of sleep was beginning to exact its toll.

She unfolded the blanket Beth had given her, laid the bundle containing food and a water bottle on the ground beneath her head, and almost immediately fell into a deep sleep, a sleep undisturbed by any dreams, let alone the nightmares she undoubtedly deserved. The nightmare was waiting for her, however, and when she opened her eyes it was there before her, straddling her thighs, its claws resting upon the thin black leather covering her breasts.

'You,' hissed Oona, 'will now be Oona's bitch.' The claws raked down, scoring the leather of Jane's britches. 'Take off,' the dog-girl growled. 'Take off, or Oona take off!'

A few minutes later, crouched on all fours, with those terrible talons closed about her tight little breasts, Jane Handiwell was given her first experience of a flesh-and-blood penis. Howling quietly in the back of her throat, Oona drove the instrument of her fall deep into her virgin pussy with a steady, unhurried rhythm. And as the razor-sharp claws moved up to encircle Jane's slender throat, it seemed her first experience was also about to become her last...

Footnotes and Fancy Frees

And so we leave our tale, dear reader, still with a few untied ends to consider. Harriet, Matilda, Kitty and Sarah, we know they all survived, but what of their future in our past, and what of Crawley, Jane, Oona, and the Graylings?

Well...

Harriet recovered from her ordeal and accepted Thomas Handiwell's proposal of marriage. With his money to pay for medicines and doctors, her father survived another twenty years, even leaving his bed to become a member of Charles II's parliament.

Her cousin, Sarah, much changed by her experiences, went back to London and became a popular actress at Drury Lane and other theatres of the time. She was even more popular amongst a certain element of the aristocracy, but over that side of her career we draw a discreet veil.

Jacob Crawley, a.k.a. Matthew Hopkins, disappeared again from the pages of history, and as we discussed earlier, faded into that obscure section of the past that is marked 'Rumour and Hearsay'. Let's hope his end, when it finally came, was not too pleasant.

And what of Jane Handiwell and Oona? Well, it is certain Jane never did inherit the *Black Drum*, for that passed down to Thomas and Sarah's eldest son, Richard, and from Richard to his son Thomas, and from Thomas to his son Richard, etc. etc. until it was eventually sold to a developer. Upon the site now stand a motorway roundabout and the branch of a popular supermarket.

There were stories in the 1660s (and for a good few decades afterwards) about two strange women who roamed the Hampshire countryside acting more like dogs than humans, killing sheep occasionally and...

Roderick Grayling became a member of the government (as Paddy Riley observed, democracy and true justice would be a long time coming, and we're probably still waiting for it now, to be honest).

Ellen married a Scottish nobleman and happily seduced each and every one of his nine sisters.

Paddy and Sean eventually went back to Ireland, although Paddy returned later to run the inn for Thomas Handiwell, and joined him in an ill-fated venture to open the first Irish theme pub in Portsmouth. Rumour has it the pub failed because there were too many genuine Irish patrons in it every night.

Jane's faithful maid, Beth, having waited in vain for her mistress at the crossroads at Petersfield for three nights, returned to the village. She spent a week getting drunk on Thomas's best wines, and then tiring of the idea of Sapphic love, she pounced upon young Toby Blaine on the evening of his sixteenth birthday. They married a few months later and lived together for over fifty years, raising five strapping sons and four daughters, one of whom went on to become the personal maid of a rather notorious duchess in London.

And that just about takes care of everyone except Ross, of the most ingenious mind. It's only a rumour, but it was reputed that his grandson sired a bastard child who went on to design a variety of intricate bridges, engines and ships that would have much pleased his great grandfather, had he lived to see them. Unfortunately, Ross met an untimely end when one of his own inventions collapsed at an inappropriate moment. His injury was only a splinter wound, but then this was before an even more ingenious mind discovered penicillin.

Who says there is no such thing as justice?

Well me, actually, but I'm just an old cynic.

Appendix I
Dramatis Personnae
(Who's who and doing what to whom and with what!)

BILLINGS, Anne - Wife of George Billings, local shoemaker. Anne works at the *Black Drum* and is recruited by Harriet to help her try to find out who and what is behind the kidnapping of her cousin, Sarah.

BLAINE, Ned - Small-time farmer and customer at the *Black Drum*.

BLAINE, Toby - Ned's teenage son. Toby poaches and knows every inch of the local countryside, and despite a lack of education is really a very intelligent young man. His friends, who help him in his quest to assist Hannah, are Matt Cornwell and Billy Dodds.

BROTHERWOOD - Senior Garrison Officer at Portsmouth, agrees to 'lend' Colonel Robert Thomas Handiwell the services of Captain Timothy Hart, a young officer who is supposed to be on convalescent leave, together with a small escort party of troopers.

CALTHORPE, Francis - Local miller and businessman.

CALTHORPE, James - Son of Francis; a scholar and would-be beau of Matilda Pennywise.

CRAWLEY, Jacob - Witchfinder. Quite possibly really Matthew Hopkins, the notorious witchfinder general from some fifteen years earlier, whose actual fate still remains shrouded in mystery. His chief assistants are Silas Grout and Jed Mardley, but he buys further help and loyalty wherever and whenever the need arises.

DIGWELL-SHORT - Ineffectual constable of the local militia, whose numbers have become depleted by the needs of the main military.

GRAYLING, Roderick - Heir to Grayling Hall and to the fortunes of his dissipate father, Earl Grayling. During his father's absence in the New World, Roderick has established a lucrative centre for slave trading at the Hall, where he enjoys the attentions of his two diminutive black slave girls, Popsy and Topsy.

GROUT, Silas - Assistant to Jacob Crawley.

HANDIWELL, Jane - Thomas's daughter. A lesbian who hates Hannah for her beauty and for the fact that her father wishes to marry her, Jane is the leader of a small band of highwaywomen and a would-be witch. Her maid, Beth, is her devoted body slave. Jane's accomplices are Kate Dawson, Mary Watling (a strapping wench built more like a man) and Ellen Grayling, Roderick's teenage sister.

HANDIWELL, Thomas - Landlord of the *Black Drum*; a widower in his early forties, Thomas has proposed to Harriet several times.

HART, Captain Timothy - Young officer on convalescent leave who is sent with a small escort party to assist Handiwell in trying to find and rescue the abducted Sarah.

HAWKIN, George - Senior overseer at Grayling Hall and steward to Sir Roderick Grayling. Among his younger staff are Young Pip (possibly his illegitimate son), William, and Ross, a tall, thin sandy- haired young man who takes Sarah's virginity shortly after her arrival.

HORROCKS, Paul - Local labourer, now deceased, he signed a testimony against Matilda accusing her of heretic practices.

MARDLEY, Jed - Assistant to Jacob Crawley and former itinerant mercenary and executioner.

MERRIDEW, Harriet - Heiress to the small farm estate of Barten Meade.

MERRIDEW, Oliver - Harriet's father and owner of Barten Meade, a former army major wounded in battle and now virtually bedridden.

MERRIDEW, Sarah - Harriet's cousin, orphaned by a plague outbreak, she travelled to Leddingham to join her only remaining family, but is kidnapped by the highwaywomen and sold to Roderick Grayling to be trained at his slave farm at Grayling Hall, a few miles from Barten Meade and Leddingham village.

PARKES, Miranda - Young girl who has fallen foul of the Grayling slave operation. Now being trained at Grayling Hall, she has been nicknamed Titty Kitty by the overseers on account of her inordinately large bosom.

PENNYWISE, Hannah - Grandmother of Matilda and reputed witch. Her late father, Nathan, was a small businessman who built up a small fortune people think Hannah must still have.

PENNYWISE, Matilda - Attractive village girl born in London and now living with her grandmother after an outbreak of Plague in the city.

PERKINS, Sam - Wagon driver who transports slaves from London and other cities to Grayling Hall.

PORTFIELD, Adam - A senior overseer at Grayling Hall.

PORTFIELD, Daniel - Adam's younger cousin, a groom/trainer at the Hall.

SLANE, John - Blacksmith in Leddingham village.

WICKSTANNER, Simon - Minister of the Church for the parish of Leddingham.

WILLETT, Dick - Coach driver on the London to Portsmouth route, wounded when Jane Handiwell's highwaywomen abducted Sarah; his assistant is Francis, a young lad of uncertain origins.

Some Important Dates in the 17th Century

1645 - Or thereabouts, because documentation is not exactly overflowing on the subject, Matthew Hopkins, former Witchfinder General, disappears from public life. One story is that he is tried and executed by an obscure rural court, another that he flees the country with his ill-gotten gains, but *we* know the truth...

1649, January 30 - Execution of Charles I - The Protectorate, under Oliver Cromwell, gets a head start.

1660, May 29 - On his thirtieth birthday, thanks largely to the machinations of General George Moncke, and the fact that Oliver Cromwell's son, Richard, has made such a miss of trying to run the country after his father's death, Charles Stuart rides in triumph into London and the monarchy is restored under Charles II. Nell Gwynne (among many others) is later also restored under him, but that is another story.

1665 - The Bubonic Plague finally reaches epidemic proportions with thousands dying daily, especially in the larger cities.

1666 - The Great Fire of London starts in a bakery in London's Pudding Lane. Sir Isaac Newton discovers the Laws of Gravity.

If you've not already read it, the prequel to **The Devil's Surrogate** is **Cauldron of Fear**, also published by us and available from **AMAZON**.

The metal contraption was an old scold's bridle, something Matilda had only previously seen in picture books at her former home. The iron bands were dull, but any rust appeared to have been removed and the hinges showed traces of having been oiled. Her initial reaction was to draw back, attempt to resist having the cruel device placed upon her head, but she quickly realised that such an action was futile and likely only to earn her even more dire retribution.

Set in the latter half of the seventeenth century, in an England ruled by fear and superstition, this is a tale of ignorance versus wealth and so-called education where, despite the fact that the notorious Witchfinder General has supposedly died in disgrace some fifteen years since, his acolytes continue his nefarious work in the more remote villages and hamlets.

Greed, torture and a clandestine white slavery network are all intertwined here, where the wrong word, a misinterpreted glance, or simply a pretty maiden spurning the advances of a powerful admirer, can lead to a gruesome death, or worse still, a life of degradation, humiliation and constant agonies.

Add a handful of genuine witches, with their own speciality of 'wyrd' sex, abduction and torture, and life in rural Hampshire starts to become more than just a little precarious.

www.ingramcontent.com/pod-product-compliance
Lightning Source LLC
Chambersburg PA
CBHW060939120626
46557CB00003B/1059